I Cannot Tell a Lie
at
George Washington
Elementary

A Novel

Jim Adolf

For more information, visit www.jimadolf.com

For Josie, Maggie and Michele

CHAPTER ONE

Everything I'm about to tell you is completely, totally true. Seriously, you can believe it all, every single word. The fact is, I couldn't lie even if I wanted to. Just a minute ago I asked myself a direct question, out loud, like I was talking to someone else. I stood in front of my bedroom mirror, looked myself in the eye, and said: "What happened that time when the truck went into the lake?" And then I started writing down the answer, everything I could remember, and I guarantee that it's all one hundred percent true. You'll see what I mean.

It all started two weeks ago, although we didn't know it at the time. My mom was sitting at the breakfast table reading the newspaper, and I was sitting with her and wolfing down a bowl of cinnamon toasties cereal so I wouldn't be late for the bus for school. My dad was in the shower and my sister Johna was upstairs too, probably putting on some black nail polish or something. To be honest

I'm not exactly sure what she was doing, but she's 13 and she's usually upstairs putting on something black, nail polish or eyeliner or army boots or whatever.

"Hey, Paulie," my mom said – that's my name, Paul actually, but my family still calls me Paulie even though everyone else has taken the hint that I like to be called Paul now – "listen to this." She turned her newspaper so I could see it. "Last night a truck went off the road on Route 4, and went plowing right into the lake."

"Uh huh," I mumbled, paying more attention to my cereal.

"I sure hope the poor guy has good insurance," my mom said, flipping the page of the newspaper. "Or the trucking company, at least."

"Who has insurance?" I asked through a mouthful of milk and chewed toasties.

"The truck driver," my mom explained. "I said I hope he has good insurance. Because of the crash. Geez Paulie, you're a zombie in the morning. Were you up late playing computer games, by any chance?"

"I take the fifth," I said. My mom taught me that – she's a lawyer, and she once told me that if someone asks you a question in court, but you don't want to answer it because you're afraid you'll get in trouble, you can say, "I take the fifth." It has something to do with the Constitution, I think she said. And I knew if I answered her question now, about using the computer late at night, I'd get in trouble. So I took the fifth.

My mom smiled and shook her head. "Okay, I'll let it slide this time," she said. "I just hope you never have to use that trick in court. I'm glad to have you as a son, but I don't ever want you as a client."

My mom's job is to defend people who've been arrested – that's who she means when she talks about her "clients." My dad always says that my mom sticks up for criminals, and he means it as a compliment, but then my mom corrects him and says that her clients aren't actually criminals unless it's been proven that they did a crime. Until then, they're just "suspects." It's one of her favorite things to lecture us about: that everyone is innocent until proven guilty, it's the American way and whatnot. When my mom corrects my dad he just shrugs his shoulders. He's a painter – not a house painter, but an artist who paints pictures – and he gets bored by all the law talk. His head is always up in the clouds, my mom likes to say.

"I don't think they'd put me in jail for using the computer," I said.

"No, you're probably right," my mom agreed.

"Do they even put nine-year-olds in jail at all?" I asked.

"Not usually. Especially perfectly obedient ones like you," she said, grinning at me. She was being sarcastic.

"Do you think they'll put the guy who drove the truck into the lake in jail?" I asked.

"It depends," my mom answered. That's always her answer when we start talking about lawyer stuff.

"Are you guys talking about the truck that went into the lake?" my sister Johna asked. She had just come into the kitchen – wearing all black, of course – and was popping a piece of whole wheat bread into the toaster. She didn't wait for Mom or me to answer. "I just heard it on the radio. Do you know that our drinking water comes from that lake?"

Now my dad came in, took a mug from the cabinet over the sink and poured himself a cup of coffee. "What are we talking about?" he asked. His hair was still wet, and he looked like he wasn't quite awake yet. He likes to work on his paintings late at night in his studio – which used to be our garage, but now doesn't even have room for our car because of all the easels and canvasses and paint and stuff – so he's always pretty groggy in the morning.

"We're talking about a truck that crashed right into the lake last night," Johna explained. "And polluted our drinking water. Do you have any idea what kinds of oil and chemicals and other bad stuff comes seeping out of trucks when they crash?"

"Actually," my dad said through a yawn, "I really don't."

"Well," Johna said, and she looked pretty annoyed, "lots of oil and chemicals and other bad stuff seeps out. Right into our drinking water."

"Don't they filter the bad stuff out of the water?" I asked.

Johna looked at me like I was a poisonous lizard that just crawled out of the sewer, which is how she looks at me usually, and rolled her eyes.

"I think Paulie's right," my dad said, rubbing his eyes. "There's a big water treatment plant somewhere, and they run all the water through it so it's clean before it gets to us. I'm sure it's safe, or they wouldn't let us drink it."

Now Johna rolled her eyes at dad. "You're so trusting, Dad. When are you going to realize that they're ruining the environment, and nobody does a thing about it?"

"Who's ruining the environment?" Dad asked. "Truck drivers who drive into lakes?"

"Very funny," Johna said.

Just then we all heard the bus coming up the street. "You guys better move it," Mom said. "If you miss the bus, you're walking. I've got an early meeting so I can't take you."

I shoveled in one more mouthful of cinnamon toasties, Johna stuck her piece of toast in her mouth, and we both grabbed our backpacks and raced out the door. We made it to the curb just as the school bus was pulling up.

CHAPTER TWO

It's kind of a funny coincidence that our town is called "Honestyville," I mean considering all the stuff that was about to happen. Our town was started by this group of settlers who bought the land from the Native Americans who were living here before them. Only unlike lots of other places where the settlers gave the Native Americans like twenty dollars or something for a huge piece of land, our settlers gave them hundreds of dollars or so, which was a fair price for the land at that time, and also let them keep living nearby. At first the town was called Lakeville, because of the lake, but the story about how honest the settlers were spread around the whole area and everyone started calling it Honestyville. Everyone in town thought that was pretty catchy, so they adopted it as the official name. That was two hundred years ago or so.

Our schools are all named after famous honest people too. I go to George Washington Elementary, and by the time you get to be in fourth grade like I am you've heard the story a thousand times about George Washington as a kid chopping down his father's cherry tree and then telling the truth about it, even though he knew he'd get punished for it. Johna goes to Abraham Lincoln Junior High, and although I haven't heard the story of why he was so honest a thousand times yet, I do know that his nickname was "Honest Abe." So it definitely fits with the theme.

I like school okay – history and math, mostly. I don't really understand why we have to learn spelling when every computer has spell checker, so you don't actually need to know how to spell words like you did a hundred years ago. My teacher, Mrs. Groom, is really into spelling, but she's pretty old and probably will retire any year now. So then it's bye-bye spelling, if you want to know my prediction. Anyway, the thing I like best about school is this activity we do after school called "Olympic Mind Games." We call it "OMG" for short.

My OMG team is me, my best friend Seth, and two girls in our class, Tibby and Analise. The girls are okay, but Seth and I probably wouldn't have chosen girls for our team at all except that Mrs. Groom said all the teams had to have boys and girls on them, equal numbers. OMG is a competition where you get a challenge that is kind of historical, and then your team has to write a short play to solve the challenge. In our case, the challenge is called

"History with a Twist": we have to take an important event that really happened in history and then imagine what might have happened if it had gone differently.   Like for example, what would have happened if the dinosaurs never died out. (One of the other teams is doing that one.)

Our topic is what would have happened if Thomas Edison had never invented electricity. Seth is really into Thomas Edison – he gets totally excited and kind of embarrassing when he starts talking about all of Edison's inventions and whatnot – and he convinced the other three of us on the team that it would be a good topic for OMG. Anyway, he's got tons of books on the subject, not to mention all this information about it in his head, so we figured at least it would give us a good start.

Our team is called "Team Electricity," which at first I thought was kind of lame. But Analise came up with it and she's pretty sensitive, so none of us wanted to tell her we thought it was corny and hurt her feelings. So Team Electricity it is, and actually my dad designed t-shirts with lightning bolts on them that are pretty cool. On the day we heard about the truck crashing into the lake, our team had been working on our play for over a month, and we had two more weeks to go. At the end of the two weeks, we'd be performing our play, along with all the other teams, in front of our parents and sisters and whoever else showed up. But most importantly we'd be performing for the judge – our Principal – who would give us all scores and decide which play was best.   The winning team gets mentioned in the newspaper and gets a trophy and medals with red-white-and-blue ribbons attached so that you can hang them around your neck. So needless to say, we all wanted to win pretty badly.

Team Electricity met at Tibby's house that day after school. We took turns meeting at each other's houses, but Tibby's was an especially good place to meet – her room was very neat, so we had plenty of space to move around, and her mom made chocolate chip cookies and let us have three each. At Seth's house we'd have to eat granola or carob chips or some other weird natural food. At my house, my dad would usually come up with some pretty good snacks, but my room was pretty messy so it was hard to find a clear space to work on our play. Analise's room was clean and the snacks were not bad, but we had to talk really quietly because her grandpa lived with them and he didn't like too much noise.   It explained why Analise always talked quietly, even when she wasn't at home – I guess she just got in the habit.   Anyway, we were at Tibby's house that afternoon, and that was a good thing.

"You know what Evan said to me today in gym?" Seth asked the three of us. Evan was a kid in our class, and he was a bit of a bully and his family was rich and he never let anyone forget it. "He said Team Dino Dogs is going to crush us at OMG." Evan's team was the one doing the play about the dinosaurs never becoming extinct.

"Who cares what Evan says," Tibby said. "He's always bragging about something."

"Well, he says Team Dino Dogs built a huge dinosaur," Seth said. "Made out of wires and plaster. Like six feet high."

"How did they have time to do that, and also finish their skit and everything?" Analise asked.

"Who knows," Seth shrugged.

"My dad could probably build a six-foot dinosaur in like two days," I said.

"We're not supposed to get help from our parents," Analise reminded us. "It's against the rules."

"I wasn't saying we should get him to do it," I explained. "I was just saying he could."

"Anyway," Tibby interrupted, "we don't need a six-foot dinosaur for our play. But we need costumes, remember?"

"Right, we decided on fake fur," Seth said. "Where can we get it?"

"They might have something at the Fabric Barn over in Mercyfield," Analise offered. "I bet my mom will take me this weekend if I ask her."

"Perfect," Tibby said.

We talked some more about our play, and decided that pretty soon we'd need to write our lines down and start memorizing them. Analise wanted us to start right away, because she was a little nervous about the whole speaking-in-public thing and wanted to get going on learning her lines. But we hadn't really finished the story yet, so we agreed we'd do that first and then get the lines down on paper next time. We worked on the storyline for a while, ate a couple of cookies, and then it was getting close to dinner time so Seth, Analise and I all agreed we probably ought to get going home.

I was the last one out the door, and Tibby grabbed the arm of my jacket just as I was about to go. "Hey, Paul," she said, and I turned around.

"Yeah?"

Tibby smiled at me, kind of a weird, nervous smile. "Never mind," she said. "I'll see you tomorrow."

"Okay," I said. Then I ran out after Seth and Analise. "Hey, wait up you guys," I shouted.

CHAPTER THREE

Here's another reason why you can believe me: I'm about to tell you about something I did that makes me look bad. There's no way you could say I'm making this all up just to make myself look like some kind of hero. Once you read this next part, you'll probably think I'm a snooping kid who reads other people's emails that he's not supposed to read. Which I guess I am. Trust me, if I didn't have to tell you about it I wouldn't. But it happened, and it's important for you to know it, so I don't have any choice. So here goes.

When I got home that afternoon, the house was quiet. I went upstairs to dump my backpack in my room and noticed that Johna's door was closed, and I could hear her creepy goth music playing inside her bedroom. Down the hall my dad's door was closed too, which meant he was taking a nap, which is what he did every afternoon at that time. Dad and I were a lot alike in this one way – we were night people, which meant we liked to stay up late, but it also meant we were pretty tired during the day sometimes. Dad liked to paint at night, and I liked to do my homework late at night. Or I guess I should say I *don't* like to do my homework in the day time, so night time is the only time left. Anyway, I definitely didn't feel like doing my homework right then, and nobody was nagging me about doing it, so I went back downstairs to the little study room off the living room, where we keep the computer.

I wasn't planning on snooping when I went down there. Seth had shown me this website called Classic Arcade Games and I was really into this old game I found there called Defender, where you drive a spaceship and shoot lots of aliens, and I was just planning on playing that for a while. But when I clicked the computer mouse, my mom's email window popped up. I guess she had been reading it before she left for work in the morning, and she forgot to close it when she was done. And just as I was moving the cursor over to the little "X" in the corner to shut it down, the title of one of my mom's new emails caught my eye. It said, "Chemical Spill in the Lake – Top Secret," and it was from one of my mom's friends from law school, Susan. Susan works as a defense lawyer, just like my mom. The email was still all in bold black letters, which meant my mom hadn't read it yet.

My hand and the mouse drifted back over toward the email, and before I knew it I had clicked on it. Here's what the email said:

Don't know if you heard, but there's a rumor going around that the truck that crashed into the lake yesterday was a tanker full of sodium pentothal. Can you believe it? Truth serum, in this day and age! And that the truck was headed to the state police headquarters to make a big delivery of the stuff. Unfortunately, there's no way to prove it now because all the truth serum drained out of the truck.

This could explain why so many clients have been making confessions lately, don't you think? – I've heard some clients claim that the police were injecting them with truth serum to get them to confess, but I didn't think it was true until now. I didn't even think that sodium pentothal really made people confess to their crimes when they were injected with it – I remember that we learned about it in law school, but didn't our professor say that it was just a crazy old method that was never really proven to work? Well, it sounds like it is working after all, and the police are filling their needles with it and forcing suspects to spill the beans. We'd better be on the lookout – just thought

you'd want to know, in case any of your clients
make surprise confessions.

Sodium pentothal? Truth serum? I'd never
heard of this stuff before, but I guess it was some
kind of secret chemical that made criminals tell the
truth. Sounded pretty awesome, actually. Just the
kind of thing that a secret agent might have in his bag
of tricks for fighting evil geniuses. I started to think
about all the cool ways I could use truth serum when
I heard my dad's door open and his footsteps come
down the hall and reach the stairs. I panicked, and I
erased the email message to my mom and closed
down the computer.

A few seconds later my dad came tromping
through the living room. "No more computer games,
Paulie," he said through a yawn. He was rubbing his
eyes and didn't stop or even look at me. "Mom will
be home any minute," he added, and then he was
gone.

"Okay, dad," I said, pretty much to nobody.

CHAPTER FOUR

The next day was when things started getting strange. Not all at once, but little by little. The first time I noticed anything was on the playground, at afternoon recess. That kid Evan – remember, the one from Dino Dogs – and three of his buddies were picking on this third grader named Martin, who was a nice enough kid but a little on the small side and definitely not good at sports. None of that so far was unusual – Evan and his gang are usually making fun of some smaller kid on the playground or pushing someone around, not so much that they'll get in big trouble but enough so that the kid they're picking on is upset or at least embarrassed.

This day was a good example. I guess the third graders were studying frontier living that month in class, and one of the projects they did was sewing their own pillows and stuffing them with straw or whatever they used back in the olden days. So a lot of third graders were walking around with these pillows they had made, even on the playground.

Evan and his buddies grabbed Martin's pillow – he was the smallish third grader – away from him and started playing keep-away with it. Then the game of keep-away turned into something more like a game of football, and they were really winging that pillow around hard and dropping it on the pavement and even stepping on it. And it wasn't like it was a pillow that you bought at the store and could take that kind of punishment, it was just a raggedy thing made by a smallish third grader. So the next thing you know, the pillow is coming apart at the seams and straw is spilling out of it all over the place and it starts looking more like a popped balloon than a pillow. Evan and his friends thought that was hilarious, and they all bent over laughing and slapped each other on the back. Poor Martin looked like he was going to cry, and then he went running back inside our school building.

Like I said, all of this was pretty normal stuff for recess. Seth, Tibby, Analise and I had made a habit of going over to the swings farthest from the pavement area and just kind of hanging out there, so we could see what was going on but not get sucked into it. Sometimes it was like a wild animal kingdom on the playground, and it was best to keep a safe distance from certain animals.

Now here comes the strange part: out of the school building comes our principal, Mr. Van Vleck, and right behind him is Martin the third grader. You can tell he's been crying, because his face is all red and his eyes are puffy. And Mr. Van Vleck has his deadly serious face on, which you can see even under his bushy grey beard. He's a pretty jolly principal usually, so it was a little bit of a shock to see him looking so mad.

Before I tell you what happened next, I should tell you a little bit about Mr. Van Vleck. He's one of the friendliest older people you'll ever meet, even though he has some habits that can get a little annoying sometimes. One of these habits is that if you ask him a question, most of the time he'll ask you one back instead of answering yours. For instance, if you were to say, "Hey Mr. Van Vleck, we don't have Salisbury steak for lunch today, do we?," he might say back to you, "Have you checked the lunch schedule in the office?" Or if you asked him, "What's the capital of Switzerland?," he'd say, "What do *you* think the capitol of Switzerland is?"

Another of his slightly irritating habits is that if you spend more than two minutes in a room with Mr. Van Vleck, it's guaranteed that he'll mention that his great great great great great grandfather was Octavius Van Vleck, one of the original settlers of Honestyville. I think I've heard him mention it probably a hundred times. He's so proud that his ancestors were the ones who gave the Native

Americans a fair price for the land and started our little town – "it was no more than a way station for horse and buggies at first," he always says – that he actually has one of those faded old black-and-white pictures of Octavius and his wife and the five Van Vleck children framed and propped up on his desk. Let me tell you, that story gets boring in a hurry.

Anyway, Mr. Van Vleck came tearing out onto the playground looking like he wanted blood, with Martin tagging along behind him. They walked right over to Martin's pillow – or what was left of it – which was lying in a heap over by the bike rack. Martin scooped it up and said something to Mr. Van Vleck, who nodded but kept that serious look on his face, and then they walked over toward Evan and his buddies, who were all the way at the other end of the playground and were pretending they had nothing to do with the destruction of the pillow.

Then Mr. Van Vleck got up really close to Evan and looked him in the eye. Evan was the tallest boy in our class, so he was only a few inches shorter than Mr. Van Vleck, and their noses were only about a foot apart.

"This young man tells me that you and your friends tore his pillow apart on purpose," Mr. Van Vleck said to Evan. "Is that true?"

Evan had kind of a half smile on his face, and he started to say something but then he stopped.

Then his eyes got kind of squinty. And instead of him saying that he had nothing to do with it, which is what every kid on the playground expected him to say, including me, he said in a low voice, "Yes, sir. Yes I did."

Even Mr. Van Vleck seemed surprised. "You did this?" he asked again, pointing to the mangled pillow.

"Yes I did," Evan said. He looked surprised he had said it himself.

Mr. Van Vleck scratched his beard.   "Why would you do such a thing?" he asked.

"I guess I wanted my friends to think I was, you know, tough," Evan answered.

"Well," Mr. Van Vleck said quietly, "at least it sounds like you're telling me the truth."   Then he turned to Evan's buddies. "And you boys," he asked, "also were part of this?"

"Yes, sir," they all mumbled.

"Well then, boys, you'll be fixing it." And with that, Mr. Van Vleck took the pile of fabric and pillow guts from Martin and led Evan and his three friends back into the school building. Sure enough, they spent the rest of the day sewing the third grader's pillow back together, and they had to stay inside for the next three days of recesses. In the meantime, the rest of us didn't know what to do. It was like we had just watched Evan and his gang have a group brain transplant. Finally, a group of third graders rushed over to Martin and started patting him on the back and cheering.   Then the rest of us joined in too, jumping around and cheering.   We weren't even exactly sure why we were doing it. It was nuts.

CHAPTER FIVE

"We can't call ourselves cavemen." That was Tibby talking. It was later in the afternoon, and we were at Seth's house working on OMG.

"Why not?" Seth asked.

"Because we're not all men. Two of us are girls."

"It's just for the script," I said, through a mouthful of organic granola cluster that Seth's mom had made and tasted like cardboard mixed with burnt onions. "Nobody will even know."

"But *we'll* know," Analise said, agreeing with Tibby. "It's not fair, even just in the script."

"Fine," Seth said, shrugging his shoulders. "I'll write down 'Cave people.' Is that better?"

"Cave *business* people," Tibby said. "That's important for the play."

Seth looked at me, and I looked back at him with an expression on my face that meant, "it's not worth fighting about, just write it down."

"Okay," Seth said, sighing.

"Good," Tibby said.

The basic idea of our play was that if electricity had never been invented, everyone in our society would still be cave people, dressed in animal skins and whatnot. Even people who worked in offices, they'd all be wearing animal skins and carrying clubs and have shaggy hair. And they would use old fashioned typewriters instead of computers, and when they brought in leftovers from dinner to eat for lunch the next day at work (like my mom does), instead of warming the stuff up in a microwave, they'd have to cook it over an open fire like they were camping out. We thought it would make for a pretty hilarious play for the four of us to be working at an office wearing animal skins, having some kind of business meeting, and then when our lunch break came we'd all cook giant turkey legs or t-bone steaks over an open fire, right there in the middle of the office. There was more to it, but we'll get to that later.

After we finished writing down our lines in the script, we starting working on our costumes and scenery. Seth and Analise stayed up in Seth's room to sew the fake animal skin fabric into Roman toga-looking outfits, and Tibby and I went down into the living room to cut cardboard and paint it. We were going to make desks that were basically just tree stumps and desk chairs that would look like big boulders, stuff like that. Then once we had them cut out, we put down a bunch of old newspapers on the living room floor and laid the cardboard on top of them, so we wouldn't get paint all over Seth's family's wood living room floor.

I was using the grey paint to do the rocks, and Tibby was using light and dark brown paint to do the tree-stump desks. She kept looking up at me, like she wanted my opinion on how her tree stumps were going. Then she finally said something, and that's when things got weird again. For the second time that day.

"Hey Paul?" Tibby said.

"Yeah?"

"I wanted to ask you something."

"Okay." I stopped painting and looked at her.

"Well," she started, "it's more like I want to tell you something."

I shrugged my shoulders. "Go ahead," I said.

"It's just that, you know," Tibby was kind of stuttering, "we've been friends since kindergarten. Before kindergarten, even. Pre-school."

"I know."

"So, I guess I just wanted to know, you know, what *kind* of friends we are."

I'm sure I looked confused, because I was confused. "I don't know what you mean," I said.

"It's just that, you know, we're friends and all," Tibby said, and I guess she thought she was explaining it, "but, I don't know, is that what we are? Friends?"

I turned and looked at her. "Tibby," I said, "you're kind of freaking me out."

"Sorry. It's hard to explain."

"What's hard to explain?" I asked.

Then Tibby made this weird face, like she was feeling her teeth with her tongue, like maybe she had a cavity or a seed stuck somewhere in there. But then she kind of relaxed and took and deep breath, and she said: "I like you. Not just as a friend, I mean. I *like you* like you."

I could feel my face going red. I wasn't sure what to say to that, so I just said, "Oh."

Tibby looked at me for a few seconds. Then she said, "So?"

I still wasn't sure how to answer, so I said, "So . . . I guess that wasn't so hard to explain after all."

"No, I guess it wasn't," Tibby agreed.

We both went back to painting. But Tibby wasn't done.

"What do you think of me?" she asked, not looking at me. "Am I just a friend, or do you like me too? In that way, I mean."

And then the weirdest thing of the whole day happened. I wasn't sure how to answer her, not just because the whole conversation was embarrassing but also because I wasn't really sure what my answer was. So as I'm sitting there thinking, I hear someone answering her. And it was me! My mouth was moving, words wcrc coming out, but it was like I had no control over it.

"I do like you in that way," I heard myself saying. "I do."

Tibby turned and looked at me and smiled. "Good," she said. "That's good."

We went back to painting. About a minute later, though, Tibby started in again.

"So, should we go to the movies together this weekend? I'm sure my mom would take us."

"I don't think so," I heard myself say. I was relieved that my mouth finally had something sensible to say, even if I had no control over it.

"Why not?" Tibby asked.

"Well," my mouth explained, "like I said, I like you and all that. But if we go out together, just the two of us, Seth and all the other kids at school will find out. And they'll totally make fun of me. And my mom will ask me a million questions about it, and that will be embarrassing. And then my dad will want to have some kind of man-to-man talk about girls and stuff, and that will be even worse."

"So," Tibby said, and her eyes got very skinny, "are you saying that getting made fun of by the kids at school, and your mom asking you questions, and your dad having an embarrassing talk with you is more important than going to the movies with me?"

This time, I knew what my mouth was going to say before it came out. If I had more time I might have said it differently, but my mouth was going before I had time to tell it what to say. "That's right," it answered. "That stuff is more important. Sorry."

"Well, then," Tibby said, but she didn't finish the sentence. And then, a few seconds later, she said, "At   least   you're   being   honest,   I   guess."

CHAPTER SIX

When I got home later that afternoon, I spent some time alone in my room, doing Legos, just to clear my head. What had just happened? I'm not someone who lies a lot – my parents have told me and Johna over and over that you should always tell the truth, even if you did something bad, because you'll always get in less trouble if you come clean. But I'm also not someone who goes around telling girls he likes them, even if it's Tibby who's asking. Why did I tell her all that stuff? Why did my mouth just blurt out the truth, even if my brain didn't want me to?

And then it hit me, like a punch in the stomach: the truth. The truth serum! That email to my mom said the truck that crashed into our lake was full of truth serum, and that it makes people confess their crimes. And Johna said we use that lake for our drinking water. So . . . was it possible that some of that truth serum was in our drinking water now? Is that why I couldn't help saying what was really on my mind?

I rushed downstairs to the computer. I clicked on Google and typed in "truth serum" and "sodium" (I couldn't remember what the official name was – I knew it was sodium something). My toe was tapping nervously on the floor as my fingers hit the keys on the keyboard – I really wasn't supposed to be Googling things without my mom or dad supervising, or at least knowing that I was doing it. But this was an emergency.

In less than a second, the results popped up. "Truth Serum," and "Sodium Pentothal" – there were tons of listings. I clicked on the first one. It was from some kind of police book, I think.

"Sodium pentothal (chemical name: sodium thiopental) is more commonly known as 'truth serum'. It is a drug that decreases certain brain functions, particularly the higher brain functions of the cerebral cortex. Some psychiatrists believe that, because lying is often complicated and requires higher brain functioning, suppression of the cerebral cortex by sodium pentothal makes it unable for the subject to lie. Thus an injection of the serum forces the subject to answer questions truthfully."

Wow. My head hurt. Maybe it was my cerebral cortex. I moved down to a section of the listing that said "Side Effects."

"The most immediate side effect of sodium pentothal is a sensation of a sour odor. Most people under the influence of the drug describe the odor as smelling like rotten onions."

Maybe that's why Seth's mom's granola bars tasted so particularly nasty this afternoon. They did have an especially oniony smell.

"What are you doing?" It was Johna, and her voice made me jump. "You know you're not supposed to be using the computer without Mom or Dad's permission."

"It was an emergency," I explained, clicking my Google search away.

"What kind of emergency?" Johna asked.

"Well," I started, "remember a couple of days ago, when that truck crashed into the lake?"

"Yeah. So what?"

"So, it turns out that the truck was full of sodium pentothal. That's truth serum. It spilled into the lake. Our drinking water."

"How do you know?" Johna asked.

"I read it somewhere," I said, trying to sound like I wasn't hiding anything. "In an article or something."

"I thought you didn't care about the toxic chemicals spilling into the lake," Johna said. "I thought you said the water gets cleaned."

"I guess I'm not so sure anymore," I admitted.

Johna looked slightly pleased, but then she frowned again. "Don't change the subject," she demanded. "I'm still waiting to hear why this is some sort of emergency for you."

"Since that crash happened," I explained, "weird things have been happening at school."

"That's because you and your friends are weirdos."

"Ha ha," I said. "No, seriously. First it happened on the playground, and then at Seth's house this afternoon."

"What happened?" Johna asked.

"People told the truth. Even if they didn't want to."

Johna looked at me like I had two heads. "So people told the truth? Big deal."

"No, it was totally strange. First that mean kid Evan in my grade admitted to Principal Van Vleck that he destroyed this third grader's craft project. Then at Seth's house, Tibby asked me a question and I . . . well, I spilled my guts. Completely. And I didn't even want to."

"What do you mean you didn't want to?" Johna asked. Thank goodness she didn't ask me what Tibby and I were talking about.

"I mean I meant not to say anything, or to change the subject or something, but instead the truth came pouring out. Like my mouth was in charge of the talking, instead of my brain."

"You really are a weirdo," Johna said.

"Don't you get it?" I asked. "It's the truth serum. It leaked into our drinking water, and now we're all saying the truth. Even if we don't want to."

"I've heard you say a lot of dumb things before," Johna said, "but I think this might be the dumbest. Seriously."

"Fine. Don't believe me," I said.

"I won't. Anyway, turn off the computer. You're not supposed to be using it." Johna turned around and made like she was going to leave, but then she stopped. "Ugh, is Mom cooking something with onions for dinner?" she asked. "It smells horrible."

A light bulb went off in my head, like in a cartoon. The smell of rotten onions, just like the article said. "Hey, Johna," I said, and she turned around.

"What?"

I focused my eyes on Johna's. Then I said, "How come you wear black all the time?"

Johna's eyebrows went up, like she was surprised, and then she made her annoyed face. It looked like she was going to say something usual, like, "Shut up, you dork," but then her face kind of went soft and her eyes got all starey. And then she said, "I wear black so that the other kids in school won't think I'm a nerd. I mean, I'm smart and I do well at math and English and everything, but if I dress in black and act moody, the kids don't notice the smart stuff as much. So I guess I hide behind these black clothes, really."

I smiled. "Thanks for the information," I said. "Very honest of you."

"That," Johna said, after a long pause, "was freaky. How did you do that? How did you get me to say all that stuff?"

"I didn't do anything," I explained. "Well, I did ask the question, but I didn't make you answer it. The truth serum did."

"The stuff that went into the lake? It made me tell the truth?"

"That's right."

Johna blinked a few times. "Wow," she finally said. "That's really freaky." Then a huge grin spread over her face. "It's also really, really cool."

CHAPTER SEVEN

The next morning, for the first time in weeks, we were all at the breakfast table at the same time: Mom, Dad, Johna and me. Nobody was talking, because we were all pretty tired and concentrating on our food. Mom and I were having cereal, as usual, Dad had made himself some sort of eggy omelet type thing and Johna was eating toast. Then my dad made this wrinkly face and looked up from his eggs.

"Hey Ellie," he said to my mom (Ellie's her name), "is there a trash bag that needs to go outside?"

"I don't think so," Mom answered, not looking up from her newspaper. "Why don't you check the pantry?"

My dad got up and walked around the refrigerator to the pantry, a big walk-in closet type of place where we keep spaghetti sauce and canned corn and stuff like that. I could hear him rattling around in there, and making sniffing noises.

"I don't see anything," he said. "But it sure smells like there's a trash bag around here."

Dad came back around the refrigerator and put his hands on his hips.

"You don't smell that, Paulie?" he asked. "It smells like rotten onions or something. Oh well."

Johna looked up at me. Her eyebrows shot up her forehead and her eyes bugged out, and her mouth was in a half-smile. I could tell what she was thinking, and I didn't even need truth serum to know it, because of the conversation Johna and I had had the night before. We had stayed up late talking about this whole truth serum business. We agreed not to ask each other any direct questions, because it would almost be like reading someone's private diary even if they didn't want you to. Also, and this is the really important part, I told her about the onion smell. I told her I knew she was under the effects of the truth serum because she said she smelled rotten onions. And now I could see she was onto Dad.

Johna watched Dad as he came back and sat down with us at the table. After a minute or so, she said, "So Dad, remember last night when I came into your room, and Mom was asleep?"

"Sure, I remember," Dad said. "It was only last night, after all."

"Well, you were watching some sort of sports show. What was it exactly?"

I looked at Johna and bugged my eyes out, but she just smiled. Dad gulped down the bite of eggs that were in his mouth. He made a face like he might say, "Oh, it was nothing important," kind of a shaky half-frown with a shrug of his shoulders. But instead his frown disappeared and his face went limp. His eyes looked glassy and glazed over.

"It was the Extreme Fighting Championship, number 24. Garth 'Mountain Man' Tookey against John 'The Killer' Miller, live from the Octagon."

Mom looked up from her newspaper. Her eyes were squinty and her eyebrows pinched in the middle. "What did you say you were watching?" she asked Dad.

"The Extreme Fighting Championship, number 24," Dad said again in a flat voice. "Garth 'Mountain Man' Tookey against John 'The Killer' Miller, live from the Octagon."

Mom folded her newspaper up carefully. "Andrew," she said slowly, and I could tell she was mad because she used my dad's actual name instead of calling him "Honey" or something, "you know I don't like you watching that kind of thing. It's so violent. Grown men beating each other to a pulp, and other grown men paying money to watch it and cheering them on. It sends a terrible message."

"I know," Dad said.

"Did you just watch it this one time, last night?" Mom asked. "Or is this a regular thing with you?"

Poor Dad looked like he wanted to jump out the nearest window, but he couldn't help answering. "I watch it most Wednesday nights," he admitted, "at 10 o'clock. That's when the heavyweight fights are on."

Mom sighed. "That's disgusting," she said. "You don't let the kids watch it, do you?"

Now Dad's face looked white as a sheet. "Sometimes Paulie watches with me," he said quietly.

Mom turned to me. "You like watching it too?" she asked.

What I wanted to say was, "Boy, it's getting late. I'd better get going to school." But instead, what I said was, "Yeah, I like watching it.   Dad and I especially like the fights when the guys bleed a lot."

Mom dropped her head into her hands. "I spend all day defending criminals," she said, "and now you're turning my own son into one."

"Suspects," my dad reminded her. "They're not criminals until they're convicted of a crime."

Mom just growled. This time I did actually manage to say, "Boy, it's getting late. I'd better get going to school."   I jumped up and put on my backpack.

"Me too," Johna said, and the two of us bolted out the door.

The bus wasn't quite there yet, so we waited outside for a few minutes.

"Nice going," I said to Johna.

"Yeah," she said, "I guess I didn't expect that to go quite so badly." She looked at me. "But you sure ratted out Dad quick, too. About watching those fights with him."

"I couldn't help it," I said. "Mom asked me a direct question. There was nothing I could do. You could have avoided the whole thing if you hadn't asked Dad about the fighting in the first place."

"I'm sure it's no big deal anyway," Johna said, shrugging her shoulders. "They'll make up."

Just then, we heard the sound of a dish smashing, and some serious shouting in the kitchen.

"Sure," I said. "No big deal."

CHAPTER EIGHT

There was practically a revolt in school that day, right before lunchtime. We were lining up in the hallway to go to the cafeteria, when some kid – I couldn't see who it was – shouted out, "What the heck are they making for lunch today? It smells horrible!"

There was a lot of sniffing by all of us waiting in our lines, and then everyone started grumbling. "It smells like they're cooking rats!" someone yelled.

"That got hit by a garbage truck!" another kid added.

"Full of rotten onions!" a third screamed.

My teacher, Mrs. Groom, who was leading our line, tried to stop the commotion. "I'll tell you what's for lunch," she shrieked. She pulled out the lunch menu and started reading it. "It says here that today's meal is 'turkey tetrazzini.' So there you have it."

I guess she somehow expected that would calm us down, but it had the opposite effect.

Someone shouted, "You mean rat tetrazzini!," and someone else starting booing, and pretty soon the entire fourth grade was booing and hissing. By the time we stormed into the cafeteria, it sounded like we might burn the place down. The lunch ladies looked terrified. One of them ran out through the side door.

A minute later, the lunch lady reappeared with Principal Van Vleck by her side. He clapped his hands twice, in that loud clap that all principals have – they must teach it at principal training – and we quieted down. "What is going on here?" he bellowed.

A tall boy from the back of the line shouted, "Whatever they're cooking, we're not eating it!"

Then a girl named Violet from our class, usually very polite and quiet, said, "It smells awful, Principal Van Vleck. It really does."

"If we eat this stuff, we'll puke!" another kid shouted.

"Or die!" someone else added.

Everyone started screaming again, and it was even louder this time than before. Principal Van Vleck clapped his hands again, and we quieted down to a murmur.

"This is ridiculous," he said sternly. "You will all take your seats and eat your lunch."

Tibby stepped forward. "But it really does smell bad," she said. "Don't you smell it, Mr. Van Vleck?"

Van Vleck started to wave off her question, but then he stopped. His eyes glazed over, and he stroked his beard thoughtfully. "I do smell it, actually," he admitted.

"What does it smell like to you?" I asked him.

He took a few deep sniffs. "It smells like rotten onions," he said. "Cooked over a dead skunk."

The same lunch lady who had brought Principal Van Vleck in from the office made a huffing sound, and another – the one who gives out milk – started to cry.

"Would you want to eat this stuff, Principal Van Vleck?" Seth asked him.

All of us were dead silent as we waited for his answer.

Van Vleck stroked his beard once more. "Not if it was the last food on earth," he finally said. He turned to the lunch ladies, who all were red in the face. "I'm sorry ladies," he said. "But whatever you're cooking really does smell putrid. Kids, take your seats. It's peanut butter and jelly sandwiches for everyone today."

Most of the kids cheered, but I noticed afterward that Van Vleck looked pretty upset. After the lunch ladies finished making about a hundred PB and Js, Van Vleck went over and talked to them. The one who was crying before had stopped now, but all four of them looked really mad. One was so ticked off she even took off her hair net, which I'm pretty sure is against thc law of thc school because if they don't wear hair nets then the lunch ladies' hair could fall right into our food, and that's a serious health problem, not to mention really gross. Van Vleck patted them on the shoulders and talked to them for a long time, and by the time he was done they all seemed to have calmed down a bit.

I watched as Principal Van Vleck started to walk out of the cafeteria. Before he left he turned and looked at us. He didn't look like his normal self, all confident and in control of everything. And he didn't look upset anymore either, or mad. His eyes went side to side, across the room and back again, watching all of us chow down on peanut butter and jelly sandwiches. He twirled the end of his beard between his fingers, and tapped his foot on the floor. It was a bizarre sight. For the first time I'd ever seen in my life, Mr. Van Vleck looked nervous.

CHAPTER NINE

Things only got worse after school. We were up in Analise's room, practicing our OMG play – quietly, so we wouldn't disturb her grandpa – and all of us were jumpy. In the scene we were working on, Seth, Analise and I were sitting in a business office having a meeting. For the actual show we'd all be in our cave-businessperson outfits of course, surrounded by oversized rocks and trees and whatnot, but that afternoon we were just in our regular clothes, sitting on Analise's bed.

Seth was our boss in the play, and we all worked for a company that made wooden clubs. (We couldn't really think of anything else that cave people would buy.) At the beginning of the scene, Seth said, "So, workers, we're going to need an extra order of wood, to make the newest batch of clubs."

Then it was Analise's line: "I'll type out the order form, boss," she said, and then she pretended to type on a big clunky typewriter. We figured we'd make one out of cardboard, and then paint it to look like it was just carved out of a big rock.

Analise finished her pretend typing and then handed the order form to Seth. "This looks perfect," he said. Then he turned to me. "Okay assistant, you'd better fax this off to the wood company."

At that point I took the paper from Seth and rolled it up into a scroll. Then I put two fingers in my mouth and whistled (quietly, of course), and Tibby came into the room from the hallway. In the real play she'd come in from offstage, and she'd be wearing a pigeon costume and a sign around her neck that said, "Fax."

"Hello Fax, my trusty carrier pigeon," I said to Tibby, patting her on the head. "Take this order form to the wood company." Then I pretended to tie the scrolled up paper onto her back.

"What are you doing?" Tibby hissed at me.

"I'm tying the order form onto your back," I said.

"That's stupid," she argued. "Just stick it in my mouth. That's how carrier pigeons carry things."

"I don't think any of this stuff is in the script, you guys," Analise said.

"Actually, that's not how carrier pigeons carry things," I told Tibby. "They have them tied onto their backs."

"Since when did you become the world's expert on carrier pigeons?" Tibby said. "They carry stuff in their mouths. It's much easier that way."

"That's dumb," I said. "They don't even have mouths. They have beaks."

"You're dumb," Tibby answered.

"Whoa, whoa, whoa," Seth said, separating us. "What's going on here?"

"He has no idea how carrier pigeons carry things," Tibby said, pointing at me. "That's what's going on."

"You're the one who doesn't know how they carry things," I said.

"Stop arguing," Analise said. "You'll wake up my grandpa."

"Sorry," Tibby said.

"What's wrong with you two?" Seth asked us. "Did you guys have a fight or something?"

"Yeah, kind of," I admitted.

"Well, what was it about?" Analise asked.

Both Tibby and I turned red. Then Tibby's eyes went glassy, and she said, "I asked Paul to go to the movies with me, like on a date. He said he wanted to, but he wouldn't go because people like you," she pointed at Seth, "would make fun of him. And his mom would ask him questions."

Seth put his hands over his ears, like his head would explode. "Too much information!" he said.

"So, you guys like each other?" Analise asked Tibby and me.

"Yeah," we both admitted.

"Oh my gosh, you guys would make such a cute couple!" she said.

"You're killing me here!" Seth moaned. "Way, way too much information!"

I explained to Seth and Tibby and Analise about the truth serum in our drinking water, and about the whole can't-lie-if-you're-asked-a-direct-question thing, and the rotten onion smell and everything. They were pretty amazed. At first Seth didn't believe it.

"Okay," I told him. "I'll try it on you. Do you still sleep with a teddy bear at night?"

Seth tried to shake his head no, but his face froze and his eyes glazed over. "Yes," he whispered.

"And what's your teddy bear's name?" I asked.

"Pookie Pie," Seth answered. I could see sweat starting to gather on his forehead.

"Pookie Pie!" Analise said, giggling. "That's so cute!"

"Now do you believe me?" I asked Seth.

"That is totally freaky," Seth said.

"I know," I agreed. "We have to be really careful. Any time you ask someone a question, you have to be ready to get the real, true answer."

"Whether you want it or not," Tibby added.

We all agreed that we woudn't ask each other direct questions, at least not unless we really had to. And then we would try to only use yes-or-no questions, so that we wouldn't be forcing each other to say too much. We were spending a lot of time together these days getting ready for OMG, and we didn't want to end up arguing all the time.

Pretty soon it was time to get going home, so we all headed for the door. Just before we walked out, Analise asked Seth to stay behind for one more minute, so Tibby and I waited for him outside. When he came out, the three of us all started walking up the sidewalk together.

About a block later, Tibby asked Seth, "So, why did Analise want you to stay behind?"

"I thought we weren't going to ask each other stuff," I protested.

"It's not a very personal question," Tibby explained. "I don't see the big deal."

"She wanted to ask me something," Seth explained.

We walked for another block in silence. Then, Tibby and I couldn't take it anymore. "What did she ask you?" we both blurted out.

Seth turned and faced us. "She asked me if I thought she was weird."

"And what did you say?" Tibby asked.

Seth shrugged. "I told her no," he said.

CHAPTER TEN

Dinner that night was painful. Mom and Dad were barely talking to each other. Like for instance, at one point my mom wanted the butter, and the butter dish was sitting right in front of my dad. But instead of asking my dad for it, my mom asked me, and I had to reach right over the table which my parents always say is rude. Plus, Johna hardly talks at all at dinner anyway, so the whole meal was quiet in a creepy way. You could hear everyone's forks and knives clinking and clanking on their plates.

Finally, after what seemed like an hour of not talking, my dad broke the silence. "This is ridiculous," he said, throwing his napkin down on the table. "Ellie, giving me the silent treatment is childish."

"Any more childish than watching some guy named Mountain Goat against John-the-Killer-Whatshisname every Wednesday night in the Octagon?" my mom said, with her mouth twisted up and her eyes squinty.

"Look, I'll admit I should have told you about it," Dad said. "But it's hardly the worst thing in the world."

"Well, I think it's pretty bad to expose Paulie to that kind of violence," Mom answered. "You have no right to do that behind my back."

"Fine," Dad said, "I made a mistake."

"Every Wednesday night," Mom reminded him.

Dad stood up. "Okay," he said, and now his voice was louder. "Are you going to sit there and tell me that you've never done anything behind my back? In the whole time we've been married?"

"What exactly are you trying to say?" Mom asked, and then she stood up too.

"You want to pretend you're perfect?" Dad said. "Well, let's take a closer look. I'll ask you directly."

"Uh oh," I said under my breath.

Dad cleared his throat. "Have you ever done anything behind my back that you knew was wrong."

Mom had this look on her face that was sort of like, "Big deal, that's all you've got?" But then her face changed. It drooped, and her eyes got wide and glassy. "It was the first year we were dating," she said quietly. "You know how I loved science fiction."

"I know," Dad said.

"Well, I was embarrassed to tell you just how much I loved it. So I hid something from you."

Dad's eyebrows went up. "What was it?"

"Do you remember that summer when I went to visit my college roommate in California?"

"Sure I do," Dad said. "Sophie, right?"

"Yes, that was her name," Mom agreed, but then she shook her head. "I didn't actually go visit Sophie that weekend."

"So who did you visit?" Dad asked.

"It wasn't really a 'who.' It was more of a 'what.'"

"Okay, you'd better explain."

"I didn't go to California at all," Mom said. "I went to Milwaukee. To the Star Trek convention."

"What's a Star Trek convention?" I interrupted.

"Star Trek was a television show I loved back then," Mom said. "Every year they had a convention – a big festival – and fans of the show would come dressed as their favorite characters. There were exhibits and lectures and the cast of the show came and signed autographs. It was pretty nerdy, I have to admit."

"Did you dress up?" I asked.

"I did," Mom said with a sigh. "I was a Klingon."

"Did you wear pointy ears, and everything?" Dad asked.

Mom's head hung down. "I did," she admitted. "Pointy ears, wig, long cape. The whole thing."

We were all silent for a moment. Then Johna spoke, for the first time all night. "Wow, Mom," she said. "I didn't know you were such a dork."

My dad shook his head. "I can't believe you've been keeping this from me all these years."

"I don't see what the big deal is," Mom said. "So I went to a Star Trek convention? So what? It's not like I hurt anybody."

"The big deal is that you lied to me," Dad said. "And then you got mad at me for not telling you about the Extreme Fighting."

"There's no way you can think those two things are the same," Mom said. "You've been letting our nine-year-old son watch a horrible, violent show every week.   All I did was go to one dorky convention."

"And lied about it for years," Dad added. "I think that's just as bad."

"That's crazy," Mom said.

"So now you're calling me crazy?"

"Ugh!" Mom said, running her fingers through her hair. "You're impossible!"

"And crazy, apparently," Dad said.

Mom shook her head and then stormed out of the room.

Dad started to pick up his plate, but then dropped it back on the table. "You two can clean up tonight," he said, pointing to Johna and me. "I'm going out." And then he grabbed his jacket and stormed out the door.

Johna and I sat there, staring at the cluttered table.

"You scrape the plates," Johna finally said, standing up. "I'll load them into the dishwasher."

CHAPTER ELEVEN

On rainy days at school, instead of having recess outside on the playground we have recess inside in the gym. Those inside recesses are basically total chaos: giant red rubber playground balls flying everywhere, jump ropes whipping around inches from kids' faces, sneakers squeaking, shouts and screams, packs of kids running around together like wolves – you get the idea. Well, the next morning when I got to school, the whole school building sounded like inside recess in the gym. It was insane.

I ran to my classroom and slammed the door shut but it wasn't much better in there. I practically bumped into two girls from my class, Violet and Victoria, who were standing near the door. Vi and Vic have been best friends as long as anyone can remember, since before kindergarten at least, and they often called each other in the morning before school so that they could wear matching outfits. They were "joined at the hip," as Mrs. Groom likes to say. But not this morning. They were screaming at each other.

"I knew it was you!" Vic shouted, jabbing her finger into Vi's chest.

"Get your hands off me!" Vi shouted back, slapping away Vic's hand.

"You'd better give it back right now!" Vic screamed.

"Or what?" Vi asked sarcastically.

"Or I'll . . . I'll . . ." Vic ran over to Vi's desk and pulled out a marbled-covered composition notebook. "I'll read your diary out loud!"

"You wouldn't."

"Yes I would."

"Give that back!" Vi screamed, lunging for the notebook.

Vic pulled away. "You give me back Fizzy, and I'll give you back your diary."

So that's what this was about. Fizzy, Vic's purple stuffed Care Bear, had been missing for a month, and no one knew who had taken it. I guess it had been Vi all along.

"I don't have Fizzy," Vi protested. "He's at home."

"Well then, I guess I'll just have to start reading your diary," Vic said.

"Don't you dare!" Vi screamed, and then she threw herself at Vic. I managed to jump out of the way just in time, before I got knocked over.

You'd think Mrs. Groom would have been over there, breaking up Vi and Vic's fight. But as I looked around the room, I noticed that there were about ten other fights, just like the one between Vic and Vi, going on at the same time. Mrs. Groom couldn't be everywhere at once. She was over in the corner by the world maps, pulling one boy off of another.

The noise in the room was ear-splitting. Seth was sitting on top of his desk, ducking out of the way of flying books and pencils, his hands clamped over his ears. I caught his eye and waved him over to me. He came running.

"This is crazy!" I shouted over the noise.

"I think my ears are bleeding," Seth complained.

"Let's get out of here," I suggested. We slipped back out through the classroom door.

It wasn't exactly less noisy in the hallway, but the noise was different: less high-pitched and screechy, more deep and rumbly. It was the sound of adults shouting at each other instead of kids. Seth and I walked down the hall and around the corner, and then we stopped. The shouting was louder now, and it seemed to be coming from the teacher's lounge. We crept a little bit closer, and then the door burst open and Principal Van Vleck came tumbling out.

His hair was all messy and sticking up, and his necktie was rumpled and sideways. He was panting, and he looked up at me and Seth.

"It's like World War Three in there," Van Vleck said, shaking his head.

"What's going on?" I asked.

Ordinarily, Mr. Van Vleck would answer my question with one of his own. I was expecting him to say something like: "Wait a minute – what are you two boys doing out in the hallway?"

But instead, Van Vleck spilled the beans. "It all started when Mrs. Gilmore asked Mr. Hellman whether her new dress made her look fat. He said yes, it did!"

"Uh oh," Seth said.

"Then Mrs. Gilmore told Mr. Hellman that his toupee was so obvious it looked like he had a dead beaver on his head. And that's when all hell broke loose."

"It's the truth serum," I said.

"The what?" Van Vleck asked.

"The truth serum," I repeated. "Sodium pento-something. A truck full of it drove into the lake a few days ago, and now it's in our drinking water."

"And so everyone has to tell the truth," Seth added. "They can't help it. If someone asks a direct question."

Van Vleck ran his fingers through his beard. "Truth serum," he whispered. "Good gracious." He looked at us. "You boys are sure about this?"

We both nodded. "One of the side effects is a rotten onion smell," I explained.   "That's why everyone's been complaining about the cafeteria."

"Good Lord," Van Vleck said, "I've smelled those rotten onions myself. I thought it was my wife's cooking."

We heard a crash from inside the teacher's lounge – it sounded like a mug smashing on the wall – and then a thump that sounded like a body hitting the floor. All three of us winced.

"I'd better get back in there," Van Vleck said, covering his face with his arm.

"Good luck, sir," Seth said. And with that, Van Vleck pushed the door of the teacher's lounge open and dashed inside.

CHAPTER TWELVE

No OMG practice that afternoon, which was a good thing because the situation was still pretty tense with Seth and Tibby and Analise and me. We needed a day to cool off. When I got home from school I could tell my dad was in his art studio in the garage, because the door was closed and I could hear his jazz music coming through. He always listens to jazz when he paints, which sounds more like random noise to me than actual music, but my dad says it "stimulates his brain." When he says weird things like that, my mom always says that Dad has an "artistic temperament." Which I think just means that he's kind of a kook.

So the jazz was a normal thing for my dad, but to be painting this early in the day definitely was not – usually he didn't even start until after dinner at the earliest, or more likely after I went to bed at eight thirty. I knew I wasn't supposed to interrupt him while he was working, but I didn't often get the chance to see him in action, so I couldn't help myself. Plus, things were still pretty rough between him and my mom, so my instincts told me I should go in and check on him.

I opened the door to the garage carefully and stepped in. My dad was wearing a ratty old button-down shirt that was smeared with paint, and he had paint all over his hands and up his arms and even on his forehead. He almost looked like a kindergartener, except that he had stubble on his face from not shaving. He had a paint brush in one hand and was staring at the canvas in front of him, which had a whole bunch of colorful squares on it. I couldn't tell what it was supposed to be a painting of.

My sneaker squeaked on the concrete floor, and my dad turned around. "Hey, Paulie," he said, reaching over to his radio and turning it off. "What's up?"

"Nothing much," I said, and then I plopped down on a stool next to where he was standing.

"Careful you don't get paint all over yourself," Dad said. "Mom would be mad."

"I won't," I said. I stared at the canvas he was working on. "So, what is this painting supposed to be?"

"It's a window pane," Dad explained. "Up really close. If you look out the window at certain times of day, like sunrise, the light gets refracted by the glass and breaks up into all these little squares. That's what I'm going for. It's kind of abstract."

"Oh," I said. "What does abstract mean?"

"It means that it's not supposed to be a realistic picture of something. It's supposed to capture the mood of the thing."

"Got it."

"So, what do you think?" Dad continued. "Do you think it captures the mood of a sunrise refracted through window glass?"

I shrugged. "I guess so. I'm never really up to see the sunrise, so I can't be sure."

"Do you like it?"

"Yeah," I said. "I think it looks pretty nice."

"Thanks." My dad sat down on the stool next to mine. "So, kiddo," he said. "What's troubling you?"

Ordinarily I would have said something like, "Nothing," or "Not much," but this time the truth just spilled out of me.

"I'm worried about you and Mom," I said. "I've never seen you this mad at each other."

Dad took off his painty shirt and tossed it on top of an old bureau that was against the wall, wiped his hands on the white tee shirt he had on underneath, and then put his arm around me. "Paulie, you really don't have to worry about it," he said. "Mom and I have been in plenty of fights before. Worse than this one."

"Like when?"

"Well, there was the time when we went on vacation and I left my keys in the front door back at the house. We had to call the police to come and take them out. Mom was really mad. And we've fought about money hundreds of times. This is nothing new, I promise you."

"I don't know," I said. "This seems worse."

"Trust me," Dad said. "We've been through much worse scrapes than this one."

We sat there silently for a minute. But my mouth wasn't quite done.

"Are you guys going to get a divorce?" I asked.

My dad looked me right in the eye, and his eyes were glassy. "Honestly, Paulie, I don't know," he said. "Your mom and I do seem a little bit out of kilter lately. But I know that I don't want to get a divorce."

"Okay, Dad," I said. I hopped off the stool. "You'd better get back to work."

"Yeah, I'd better," he agreed. "But I'm happy for the interruption."

Upstairs, Johna's door was closed too, and just like Dad she had music coming through. Hers was much louder, though, and definitely not jazz – it was some kind of old rock music, like from the sixties, and the singer's voice sounded deep and warbly. I knocked on the door a few times but she didn't hear me, so I turned the knob and went in.

Johna was at her desk doing homework. I said, "Hey," but she didn't seem to hear, so I said "Hey" again, louder this time. Johna turned and looked at me.

"What do you want?" she shouted over the music.

I plopped myself down on the edge of her bed. "Can I talk to you?" I asked.

"Sure." Johna turned down the music.

"How can you do your homework with that loud music on anyway?" I asked.

"It stimulates my brain," Johna said, and we both laughed. "So what's up?"

"I'm worried about something," I said.

"What is it?"

"I'm afraid Mom and Dad are going to get a divorce."

Johna shook her head. "Paulie, that's stupid," she said. "They're not going to get a divorce."

"How do you know?" I asked.

Johna sat down next to me. "You probably don't remember this because you were too little," she explained, "but one time a few years ago Mom and Dad had a garage sale, in the summer. Dad was off doing something, getting more stickers or whatever, and Mom found a dusty old painting in the back of the garage. So she put it out on a table with all the rest of the junk, and somebody bought it for like five bucks."

"Was it a famous painting or something?" I asked.

"Not exactly," Johna explained. "But it was a painting that Dad's art teacher had made, and then given to Dad as a present when he finished art school. So it was like a sentimental thing, and also kind of Dad's good luck charm."

"That's bad," I said sucking in my breath.

"It really was," Johna continued. "Dad was so mad he didn't talk to Mom for like a week. He wouldn't even look at her. And Mom couldn't remember who she sold the painting to, so they couldn't try to get it back. And Dad's old art teacher was already dead, so they couldn't get another one. It was bad news all around."

"So then what happened?" I asked.

"Nothing happened. After a week or so they kind of made up, and that was the end of it. See my point?"

"Not really," I admitted.

"The point," Johna said, "is that if Mom and Dad didn't get a divorce over Mom selling Dad's most cherished painting, they're not going to get a divorce because Dad lets you watch extreme fighting or Mom went to a dork convention once. Get it?"

"I guess." I stood up. "Thanks, Johna."

"No problem."

I started to head for the door, but then I stopped. "I'm glad you're around," I said.

"Don't get all creepy," Johna said, rolling her eyes.

"Hey Johna," I said, "one thing before I go: are you glad I'm around too?"

Johna's face went limp. "Yes," she said, sighing. "Yes, I am."

"Thanks," I said, grinning. Then I got out of there as fast as I could.

CHAPTER THIRTEEN

I thought about wearing earplugs to school the next day, because I expected it would be loud and crazy again. But when I got there, it was the exact opposite: it was dead silent. Kids were tromping around the hallways like zombies, with their mouths clamped shut. I'm not sure they knew exactly what was going on with the sodium pentothal in the water, but everyone seemed to know that practically every time you opened your mouth, something came out that you wish hadn't. So they were trying their best not to say anything at all. It was eerie.

Inside my classroom was no different. The room had a kind of scuffing sound, as all the kids took notebooks and lunchboxes out of their backpacks and put them away, but no one was saying a word. Mrs. Groom looked totally rattled, with dark circles under her eyes and random strands of hair sticking out of the tight bun at the back of her head.

"Okay class," she said in a hoarse whisper, "everyone take out your math notebooks. We're going to do some long division practice. Quietly."

All the kids reached in their desks and pulled out their notebooks, their mouths still shut tight. No one even mumbled or groaned, which is what everyone usually does when Mrs. Groom tells us we're going to practice long division.

"Before we start," Mrs. Groom said, "I need a volunteer to take the attendance book down to the office."

Ordinarily, half the class would jump at the chance to take a trip out of the classroom, particularly during math. But this time not one kid raised a hand. And I didn't either – I saw what was going on in the teacher's lounge the day before, and I didn't want to walk into something like that in the office. A kid could get hurt.

"Anyone?" Mrs. Groom said, sounding more desperate. I guess she didn't want to go to the office either. "Please?"

The silence was painful. Finally, after about ten seconds, I couldn't take it anymore. I raised my hand. "I'll go," I said.

"Oh thank goodness," Mrs. Groom said, letting out a deep sigh. She handed me the attendance book, and I tucked it under my arm and went out the door.

When I got to the office, it looked like everyone in there had all just been to a funeral. The school secretary, Ms. Gleason, was red-cheeked and was dabbing at her eyes with a tissue. This was really strange considering Ms. Gleason had worked at George Washington Elementary for something like thirty years, and not once in all that time had she changed her facial expression – never a smile or a frown, just the same super-serious, intense stare, like she was giving you the stink eye. Most kids immediately confessed to whatever bad thing they had done when they saw Ms. Gleason's stink eye expression, so I wasn't sure how this whole truth serum business would have affected her anyway.

"What's going on?" I asked in a whisper. I didn't want to talk in a normal voice, just like you wouldn't want to talk in a normal voice if you wandered into a funeral parlor.

"It's Principal Van Vleck," Ms. Gleason said, sniffling. "He didn't come to school today." She said this in the same sad tone of voice you might use if you said, "He got eaten by an alligator."

"What's wrong with him?" I asked.

Our school guidance counselor, Mr. Lewis, who was sitting next to Ms. Gleason and had his arm around her shoulders, answered. "We don't know," he said in a whisper that I could barely hear. This was not so unusual – Mr. Lewis always spoke in a very calm, smooth whisper, like the way you might talk to a crazy person or some hyper kid who you were afraid would smash something or barf if you talked too loud. "That's the problem," he added.

"What's the problem?" I asked.

"Mr. Van Vleck has only been absent one day in the eighteen years he's been at George Washington," Ms. Gleason said, starting to sob. "That was when he had emergency surgery to remove his appendix.   And even then, he called us from the hospital waiting room before they wheeled him in for his surgery. This time," she said, and now her voice was starting to break up, "he hasn't called."

"Maybe he just overslept," I said hopefully. "Did you try calling his house?"

"No answer," Ms. Gleason said, and now she was really crying.   "We even sent one of the bus drivers over there to see if he was home.   Nobody was there, and his car was gone."

Mr. Lewis patted her shoulder gently. "There, there, Edna," he said quietly. "I'm sure Mr. Van Vleck is all right."

"Oh, are you?" Ms. Gleason snapped. "Are you really sure he's all right?"

Mr. Lewis' face fell.   "No," he admitted, "I'm not. For all I know he's dead in a ditch at the side of a road, somewhere."

"Oh, for heaven's sake!" Ms. Gleason said in between sobs.

I took the attendance book out from under my arm and laid it down on the desk in front of her. "Well, I'd better get back to class," I whispered, backing slowly out of the office.

CHAPTER FOURTEEN

That afternoon OMG practice was at my house, and we didn't exactly get a whole lot done. We were all kind of freaked out about Principal Van Vleck not coming to school. Everyone had been talking about it all day, wondering what might have happened to him. It was all we could talk about too.

"Maybe his beard got caught in an escalator," Seth said. He was sitting on the floor at the foot of my bed, in his fake-fur toga. "I saw that happen in a cartoon once. The guy got sucked right into it at the top, and then came out the bottom flat as a pancake."

"That's the dumbest thing I've ever heard," Tibby said.

"It could happen," Seth protested.

"Sure – in a cartoon," Tibby said. "Not in real life."

"Says you," Seth said, in a "nanny-nanny-boo-boo" kind of voice.

"You're so immature," Tibby responded.

I jumped in, to keep them from killing each other. "I'm sure if he got sucked into an escalator, we would've heard about it. It would be on the news or something."

"Maybe it has something to do with all this truth stuff going on," Analise said.

"Like what?" I asked.

We were all quiet for a minute.

"I've got it!" Seth said. "Maybe Van Vleck did a crime when he was younger, like twenty years ago or something, and now because of the truth serum he went to the police and confessed and so he's locked up in jail!"

"That's as stupid as your last idea," Tibby said.

"Yeah," I said, "I can't imagine Van Vleck ever doing a crime. He's too goody-goody."

"Maybe he's always been in love with a mysterious stranger," Analise said. "And he was forced to tell her his feelings, and she had to tell him that she loved him too, and then they ran off to Paris or somewhere."

"Gross," Seth said. "Don't make me puke."

"Or maybe," I said, standing up, "Van Vleck's such a goody-goody because he's actually a secret agent for the government. And maybe when he got the truth serum in him he was forced to tell someone his secret identity. So then he had to go into hiding, or else the criminals he's been spying on would try to kill him."

"That would be awesome!" Seth said, jumping up from the floor. His foot got caught in the armhole of his fake-fur toga, and we heard a loud ripping sound. When we all looked over at Seth, his toga was torn into several pieces and hanging off his shoulders.

"Nice move, spaz," Tibby said.

"No big deal," Seth said. "I can just make another one. We've still got time before the show."

"But we're out of material," Analise said.

"Can't we get more?" I asked.

"I guess so," Analise said. "I'll ask my mom if she can take us to the fabric store in Mercyfield tomorrow after school."

The sound of the front door slamming downstairs made us all jump. "I guess my mom's home," I said.

"Wow," Analise said. "Does she always slam the door that hard? My grandpa would have a heart attack."

"Not always," I explained. "Just for the last few days."

"Paul's mom and dad are in a fight," Seth said.

"That's none of our business, Seth," Tibby said. "You shouldn't just talk about Paul's parents like that. Maybe he doesn't want everybody to know."

"That's all right," I said. "I don't mind."

"What are they fighting about?" Analise asked.

"It's this whole truth serum thing," I explained. "My dad admitted that he watches extreme fighting with me sometimes, which made my mom really mad."

"Ugh, extreme fighting is horrible," Analise said. "I don't know how you stand it."

"That's pretty much what my mom said," I continued. "But then my mom admitted that one time like fifteen years ago she lied to my dad, so he got mad back at her."

"What did she lie about?" Tibby asked.

"She told my dad she was going to visit a friend," I said, "but really she was going to some kind of Star Trek thing. In Wisconsin, I think."

"Cool," Seth said. "Star Trek is awesome. I watched a marathon of like eleven episodes in a row on TV once. What kind of thing was it?"

"A convention," I explained. "Where the actors from the show sign autographs and stuff."

"Wow, I wish I could go to that," Seth said.

"Well, if it was fifteen years ago," Tibby said, "I think it's probably over by now."

"Ha ha," Seth said, and then he stuck his tongue out at her.

"Listen you guys," I said, "I get enough fighting with my parents these days. If you're going to keep arguing, maybe we should stop for the day."

"That sounds like a good idea," Analise said. "Everyone's grumpy anyway."

"Sorry, Paul," Tibby said.

"It's okay," I told her. "I'm just worn out I guess."

"No problem," she said. "We'll all meet up tomorrow after school and get material for Seth's costume. Then we can start up practicing again."

"Sounds like a good plan," I said.

Seth opened my bedroom door, and we could hear the muffled sound of my parents arguing downstairs in the living room. Seth looked back at me, and I shrugged.

"Well," he said, "maybe we'd better go out the back door."

"Good idea," Tibby said.

"Come on," Seth whispered, stepping carefully out into the hallway. "I know the back way. Follow me."

CHAPTER FIFTEEN

Mom and Dad gave each other the silent treatment at dinner that night. It was awful. We were eating pizza, because nobody was in any mood to cook. That wasn't the awful part – I love pizza, especially with pepperoni and extra cheese. The awful part was that after arguing all afternoon, my mom and dad were now pretending each other didn't even exist.

"Paulie," my dad said, "would you please pass me the milk?"

"It's sitting right in front of Mom," I told him. "Why don't you ask her?"

"Because I don't want to," Dad answered, like he was a five year old. "Besides, you can reach it."

I reached over in front of Mom and grabbed the carton of milk, and then plunked it down in front of Dad.

"Thank you," he said, smiling a kind of sarcastic smile. My mom snorted.

"Hey Johna," Mom said, nodding toward one of the pizza boxes. "Would you like the last slice of olive and spinach?" That was my dad's favorite kind, and Mom knew it.

"No thanks," Johna said.

Dad glared and Mom, and she shrugged like she couldn't even see him. "All right then, I guess I'll have it." She reached over and slowly took the slice out of the box, holding it up in the air so my dad could get a good look at it before she put it down on her plate. "I'm not really hungry anymore," Mom said, "but I've always got room for one last piece of olive and spinach pizza."

Dad's rolled his eyes. "I hope you choke on it," he mumbled under his breath.

"That's it!" Johna said, throwing her napkin down on the table. "This is totally stupid, and I've had enough."

Johna stood up, and she looked like she might throw something. "What are you going to do?" I asked.

"I didn't want to have to do this," she said, looking at Mom and then Dad. "But I guess I don't have any choice. I'm calling a family meeting."

"You can't call a family meeting," my dad said. "Only parents can do that."

"Well, considering you two are acting like babies instead of parents," Johna answered, "I think I can. What do you think, Paulie?"

"I agree," I said.

"Good. Family meeting in the living room, in five minutes," Johna said, and then she pointed at Mom and Dad. "And you two babies better be there."

Mom and Dad sat on opposite sides of the living room, Dad on the couch and Mom in the big brown lounge chair, not looking at each other on purpose. I sat on the couch near Dad, and Johna stood up by the mantle. She clapped her hands twice to get our attention.

"All right everyone," Johna said, "Let's get started. I think we all know the reason I've decided to call this family meeting." She paused for Mom or Dad to say something, but they stayed quiet.

"It's because of all the arguing," I finally said.

"Exactly," Johna agreed. She looked at Dad and then Mom. "So, which one of you two wants to explain yourself first?"

"He started it," my mom said, jerking her head in my dad's direction. "Maybe he should go first."

"That's not helpful, Mom," Johna said.

"That's fine," Dad said. "I'll be the better person and go first. But for the record, I didn't start anything."

"Oh," Mom said sarcastically, "so I suppose you didn't watch extreme fighting with Paulie?"

"Stop that right now, Mom," Johna scolded her. "You wanted Dad to go first, so he's going first. You'll get a turn in a minute."

Mom frowned and sunk down in her chair.

"Thank you, Johna," Dad said.   "So, what exactly am I supposed to say?"

"You're supposed to explain to the whole family why you did what you did, and how you feel about it now," I said. "That's what Mr. Lewis always tells us at school when we have a problem."

"Fine," Dad began.   "I let Paulie watch extreme fighting with me, because, well, it's nice for me to have some father-son time with him, just the two of us, alone.   And I think that sometimes kids feel like they don't have a way to express their anger, and watching a violent sport can be a good outlet.   I remember feeling that way as a kid, and my dad and I would watch boxing together.   So it didn't seem like such a bad thing."

"And how do you feel about it now?" Johna asked.

"I guess I feel bad that I didn't tell your mother about it, or discuss it with her first," Dad admitted. "I should have done that, I suppose."

"Very good," I said.   "So Mom, what do you think about what Dad said?"

Mom sighed. "I guess he made some good points," she said. "And I'm glad he understands that he should have talked to me about it first."

"Excellent," Johna said. "Now we're getting somewhere. Okay, Mom. Your turn. What you did and how you feel."

"I went to a Star Trek convention many years ago," Mom explained, "and I told your dad a little white lie about it because I didn't want him to think I was a total nerd."

"And how do you feel about that?" I asked her.

"I guess I feel bad that I never told him. I shouldn't have lied in the first place, and I should have told Dad the truth later on."

"Well done, Mom," Johna said. "So Dad, what do you think about what Mom said?"

"I appreciate that she understands she shouldn't lie to me," Dad said, nodding. He stood up. "I'm glad we've cleared the air between us. This was a good idea Johna, after all. And now that everything's even, we can forget about it all and get back to normal."

"Hold on a minute," Mom interrupted. "I never said everything's even."

"Huh?" Dad said, looking at her. "What did you say?"

"Uh oh," I mumbled.

"I said we're not even," Mom repeated. "I admit that I shouldn't have lied to you, but that was just a little thing between the two of us. What you did involved our son, and you have no right to make decisions about what's best for him – or for Johna -- without talking about it with me first. We're both their parents."

"But you said you thought I had a good reason," Dad said.

"I said you made some good points. But I don't necessarily agree with them. And anyway, that doesn't change the fact that you shouldn't have made the decision without me. That still was worse than what I did."

"This is so like you," Dad said, glaring at Mom. "You can't ever just leave things alone once we sort them out. You always have to win. You're such a . . . such a . . ."

"Don't say it, Dad," Johna warned.

"Such a . . . lawyer!"

Mom stood up. "You take that back!" she shouted.

"I won't!" Dad said. "Just once I'd like you to leave your lawyer personality at work where it belongs, and not try to argue us all to death at home."

"And just once," Mom said, "I'd like you to get a little bit of common sense into that flaky artistic brain of yours!"

"Stop it!" Johna shouted. "I've heard enough out of the two of you. Mom," she said, pointing at her, "you go to your room right now. You need to think about what you said and cool off."

"But I –" Mom started to say.

"No more back talk. Move it!"

Mom got up in a huff and marched up the stairs.

"And you," Johna said, turning to Dad. "You go to your studio."

"Can't I –" Dad started to ask.

"No you can't!" Johna said. "Whatever it is, forget it. Go to your studio. Now!"

Dad frowned at Johna and then went off to the garage. It was quiet for a minute, and Johna and I looked at each other.

"Great family meeting," I said.

"Oh, shut up," Johna answered.

CHAPTER SIXTEEN

Still no sign of Van Vleck the next day at school. Ms. Gleason, the school secretary, was having a panic attack or a nervous breakdown or something, which meant that she spent the whole day crying, and when she wasn't crying, she was just staring straight ahead and mumbling to herself. Mr. Lewis had to hang out with her in the office and take care of her like he was her personal guidance counselor, which meant he didn't have any time for the kids who needed help because they were homesick, or in a fight with a friend, or freaked out because their parents were getting divorced or whatever. Basically, George Washington Elementary was a mess.

After school, Seth, Tibby, Analise and I waited outside by the bike rack for Analise's mom to pick us up and take us to Mercyfield to buy more fake fur. Like everybody else in school, we were talking about Principal Van Vleck.

"He better show up for the OMG performances," Seth said. "He's supposed to be the judge."

"Don't be so selfish," Analise scolded him. "What if he's hurt or something? You're more worried about OMG than whether Mr. Van Vleck is okay."

"I'm not saying I don't care if he's hurt," Seth protested. "I'm just saying we need him for OMG. And it's only three days away."

"I'm sure he's not hurt," I said, "and I'm sure he'll be there at OMG. Van Vleck isn't going to let us down. He never has before."

"I sure hope you're right," Tibby said quietly.

Analise's mom pulled up in her minivan, and we hopped in. It was a quick ten-minute ride to the block on Main Street in Mercyfield where the fabric store was. When we got there, Analise's mom pulled the van to a stop right in front of the shop.

"I just need to run to the pharmacy for a minute," she told us, in her usual super-quiet voice. It always felt like she was telling us a secret. "Will you kids be okay in there by yourselves?"

"We'll be fine, Mom," Analise said, her voice also barely more than a whisper.

"Great, I'll see you in a few minutes," Analise's mom said, and the four of us climbed out the side door of the minivan.

The fake fur was on a shelf at the back of the fabric store, but Analise knew exactly where it was. The woman who ran the store unrolled three yards of the fabric on a big square cutting table, cut it off the roll with a little knife with a round blade and a wooden handle, and then stuffed the material into a plastic bag. Analise handed her the money for it, and we were back outside the shop seconds later. The whole thing took about two minutes.

Naturally, Analise's mom wasn't back yet with the van. We sat down on the stoop of the fabric store and waited, not wanting to go too far – if we weren't right where we said we'd be, Analise's mom would freak out.   She wasn't too good at handling unexpected things.

Directly across from us on the other side of Main Street was the Mercyfield Diner, one of those old-timey looking restaurants with metal sides that looks like a train car. A man came out of the front door wearing a tan trench coat and the kind of floppy hat you might wear to go fishing in. Seth jumped up from the stoop.

"Look everybody!" Seth said in a shouting kind of whisper, pointing at the myserious man. "Look who it is!"

We all looked.

"He just looks like some guy," Tibby said. But just as she said it, the man turned his head and we all got a glimpse of his full beard, poking out above the collar of his coat.

"It's Principal Van Vleck," Analise breathed.

We all ran across the street toward him. Van Vleck saw us coming and looked like he might run himself, his head turning back and forth to find a good route to escape, but then he just shrugged his shoulders and waited for us to catch him.

"What are you doing here?" I asked him, panting from the run across the street.

"I'm having dinner," Principal Van Vleck replied.

"At four o'clock in the afternoon?" Seth asked.

Van Vleck sighed. "I like to beat the evening rush," he explained. "There are very few people in the diner at this time of day."

"So you don't have to see anybody," Tibby guessed.

"I suppose so," Van Vleck admitted.

"But what's going on?" Analise asked. "Why haven't you been in school?"

"Yeah," Seth joined in. "Why are you hiding from everyone?"

Van Vleck sighed, and then he took off his hat. "It's because," he said slowly, fiddling with his hat, "I have a secret. Something I don't want anyone to find out."

"And you're afraid someone will ask you," I guessed.

"That's right," he admitted. "And until the sodium pentothal is out of our drinking water, I'd have to answer it. Honestly and completely. And, I'm embarrassed to say, I'd rather not have to do that."

"But," Seth started to say, "what's your big secre--"

I slapped my hand over his mouth. "Don't!" I yelled. "Don't ask him a direct question about it." I looked at Van Vleck, standing there with his hat twisting in his hand. "He'll have to say it, and he doesn't want to."

"Thank you for understanding," Van Vleck said.

"Fine," Seth said, pulling my hand away from his mouth. "I won't ask. On one condition."

"And what condition is that?" Van Vleck asked.

"You have to promise you'll show up for the OMG performance."

Van Vleck sighed once more.

"Come on, Mr. Van Vleck," Analise pleaded. "We need you there. You're supposed to be the announcer. And the judge."

Van Vleck looked at each of us, one at a time. "I suppose I made a commitment to be there," he said. "So I will keep my commitment."

"So you'll come?" Tibby asked.

"Yes," Van Vleck said, giving us a small, tired smile. "I'll be there."

"Yes!" Seth said, pumping his fist.

We heard a car horn honk from across the street. It was Analise's mom's minivan.

"Uh oh," I said. "We'd better go."

We all started to run back across the street. Van Vleck stayed where he was in front of the diner and watched us go. As we climbed through the side of the van door, Seth yelled out, "See you at OMG!"

Van Vleck waved at us as we pulled away.

CHAPTER SEVENTEEN

The next few days were a blur of rehearsals, costume sewing, cardboard painting and generally getting ready for OMG. We practically spent all our time at Tibby's house – she had a finished basement that was perfect for practicing our skit – which was great for me because I didn't have to hang around at home with my fighting parents.

But things weren't exactly perfect between me and Tibby either, so being at her house was a little uncomfortable too. I guess she was still mad about what I said when she asked if we could go to the movies. And the dumb thing was that I told her I did want to go – I just didn't want everyone else talking about it. The whole thing was just so messed up.

It was Sunday around lunch time when Tibby and I were alone for the first time. We had taken a break from rehearsing, and Analise was helping Seth finish sewing his costume upstairs. Tibby and I stayed down in the basement to finish up painting the scenery. The whole day it felt like she had been avoiding me, or at least avoiding talking to me. And so now we were standing there, painting giant cardboard sheets side-by-side, not saying anything. It was driving me crazy. I decided I had to at least try to fix it.

"Hey Tibby," I said. "You know I really do want to go to the movies sometime. With you."

"Yeah," Tibby said, shrugging her shoulders. "You said that."

"Well, I do," I said. "Still."

"Great."

"It's just that I don't want everyone making fun of me," I explained. "It's not because of you or anything."

"You said that too," Tibby answered.

I stopped painting and looked at her. "What about this," I suggested. "What if we go to the movies. You know, together, the two of us. But we don't exactly have to tell everyone about it."

Tibby turned to face me too. "So you want to go out with me," she asked, "but you're too embarrassed about it for anyone to know? Is that what you're saying?"

"No," I said, shaking my head. "I'm not saying I'm embarrassed. I like you. I really do. I just don't want people to make a big fuss about it." I went back to painting. "Can't you understand that?"

Tibby sighed. "Fine," she said. "But I want to be able to talk to Analise about it. She's my best friend. Can't I do that?"

"Sure," I said. "But can you just tell her to, you know, kind of keep it between her and you? And not go around telling the whole school?"

"Yeah, I guess I could do that," Tibby agreed.

"Good," I said. "So then maybe next weekend? We can go?"

Tibby kept painting, but I could see that she was smiling a little. "Okay," she said.

A minute later, Tibby stopped. "Even if you don't tell Seth," she said, "he'll find out, you know. He's your best friend."

"Yeah," I agreed. "I guess I'll tell him."

"And then he's going to make fun of you," Tibby added.

"Yeah, I know."

"You don't care?" She asked.

"No, I do care," I said. "But I'll get over it."

CHAPTER EIGHTEEN

We all watched from the opening in the curtain as people filed into the auditorium. It looked like about a million people were coming in – parents, brothers and sisters, grandparents and aunts and uncles. My stomach felt like it had gotten hard and was stuck just below my throat, and my hands were all sweaty. Seth's face was really white and his eyes were moving all over the place. Tibby kept giggling even though nobody had said anything funny, and Analise was kind of whispering to herself quietly, so quietly that none of us could hear what she was saying. We were really, really nervous.

One of the parents – someone I didn't recognize – was fanning his face with his hand as he walked into the auditorium. "Geez," he said loudly, "it smells like rotten onions in here!"

"Yeah!" someone else in the crowd shouted. "What the heck are they feeding our kids in this school?"

There were a few more shouts and complaints but then the commotion died down and mostly people were laughing and finding their seats.

"This could be a pretty tough crowd," I said. Tibby giggled like a crazy person. Analise whispered to herself.

Evan and his gang were backstage too, hanging out by the side door of the stage, and they didn't look nervous at all. They weren't yet in their costumes because their skit wasn't until the end of the show. We were scheduled to go second, so we were already dressed in our togas.

Evan strolled over to the four of us. He was wearing his team's tee shirt – each team had shirts made up, and naturally Dino Dogs' were the fanciest. They had the team name sewn on the front and then a picture of an animal that had a dog body but a dinosaur head. I had to admit they looked pretty cool. Our tee shirt was cool too – with the lightning bolt and "Team Electricity" spelled out across the chest – but all the letters were ironed on instead of sewn on, so they looked cheaper than the Dino Dogs'. But right now they were underneath a layer of fake fur, so you couldn't really see them anyway.

"Nice costumes," Evan said, motioning at us with his chin. "What did you do, shave a bunch of gorillas and use their hair?" His gang laughed at that, like it was the funniest thing they ever heard.

"It's fake fur," Analise whispered.

"It figures," Evan said.

"What do you mean, it figures?" Seth said.

"I mean you guys are a bunch of fakes," Evan said. "Because Team Dino Dogs are the real deal. And we're going to win a real trophy tonight."

Seth rolled his eyes. Tibby giggled.

"Good luck . . . losers," Evan said. And then he walked back to his team.

"What a jerk," Analise whispered.

"Who cares about him?" I said. "We've got to focus on our play."

Just then the audience quieted down, not completely, but so that it sounded like everyone was kind of grumbling quietly. The crowd coming through the auditorium entrance stopped and then parted in the middle, opening up a kind of tunnel, and through it walked Principal Van Vleck.

I heard a shriek from the side of the auditorium. I looked over just in time to see Ms. Gleason crumple like all the bones in her body had gone soft, and Mr. Lewis catch her. All the papers she had been carrying – the OMG score sheets, I guessed – went flying in the air.

Mr. Van Vleck jogged over to her and helped Mr. Lewis haul her back up to her feet. Then he said something in her ear and she smiled and the color came back into her cheeks. Van Vleck patted her on the arm a few times and said, "Are you sure you're okay?" Ms. Gleason said she was, and then Van Vleck made his way down the aisle and up the steps onto the stage.

Van Vleck stepped up to the microphone stand and cleared his throat. "Welcome everyone," he said, "and thank you for being here. I ... uh ... I apologize for not being around lately . . ." his voice trailed off. He opened his mouth like he was going to say something else, but then he shut it again. And then he smiled. "I could say more," he continued, "but you didn't come here to hear me talk. You came here to see the kids perform. So let's get on with the performance!"

The audience cheered and Mr. Van Vleck got off the stage quickly and took a seat right in the middle of the front row. Tibby, Analise, Seth and I scurried over to the side of the stage out of sight, just as the curtains opened.

The first team was just horrible. I know that sounds mean, but I can't help it – I have to tell the truth. Their basic idea was what would have happened if movies and TV had never had been invented, which wasn't all that interesting a theme to begin with if you ask me. Their skit took place on a rainy day, and basically all they did was sit around talking about how bored they were and how they wished they had something to do other than read or play board games. Even their team name was lame: Team Movie Stars. It didn't make sense at all, considering the whole point of their skit was that there were no movie stars, because movies hadn't been invented.

The audience clapped for them, because it was all parents and other relatives and they were being polite, but you could pretty much tell that no one thought it was very good. Tibby and Seth and Analise and I were getting pretty excited because we knew our show would be better. We were mainly going for laughs, which we thought the audience would appreciate.

We were right. When the curtain opened, Seth and I were sitting at our desks wearing our fake-fur togas, typing on typewriters. Already the audience started laughing. The first line was Seth's.

"How many wooden clubs have we sold this month?" he asked.

"I don't know, boss," I said.

"Well," Seth said, "go check the computer."

I walked over to the side of the stage to a large cardboard box, painted to look like wood. Analise was hiding inside.

"Computer," I said to the box, "how many wooden clubs have we sold this month?"

Analise popped out of the box, wearing her fur toga and holding a scroll of paper. "Four hundred and sixty nine," she said in a flat, computery voice. Her voice was strong and not wavery at all, which surprised me.

"Thank you, computer," I said.   Analise scrunched back down into the box and closed the top over her. The crowd totally cracked up.

I walked back to my desk. "Four hundred and sixty nine, boss," I said to Seth.

"That's a problem," he replied. "We promised we'd ship an order of two hundred to Joe's Wooden Club Shop. But if we already sold that many, we don't have enough left to fill the order. We'd better get more wood."

"No problem, boss," I said. "I'll send a fax off to our wood supplier." I pretended to type on my typewriter for a minute. Then I pulled the sheet of paper out of the typewriter and rolled it into a scroll. Finally I put two fingers in my mouth and whistled as loud as I could.

Tibby came running out from backstage in a full pigeon costume – basically fake feathers all over, two wings and a tail made of poster board with feathers glued on, and a giant poster board beak strapped onto her face. She was still giggling a bit, but she stopped by the time she reached me. She stepped in front of me and did a salute with one of her wings.

"Fax, here," she said, "at your service."

The crowd went crazy, laughing and clapping.

"Hello, Fax," I said to her, handing over the typed scroll. "Take this to our wood supplier."

Tibby took the scroll and put it in her fanny pack, which she was wearing around her waist. For some reason, this made the audience laugh even harder.

"Yes, sir," she said, saluting me one more time and then heading off stage, flapping her wings as she went.

In the next part of our skit, all four of us were in a business meeting wearing our togas. Analise and Tibby were giving a presentation, and although they said it was "PowerPoint," it really was just Tibby holding up a bunch of pictures on poster board. We had drawn the pictures with crayons and made them look like four year olds had done them, and that got another big laugh from the crowd. Then we all said we were hungry, and Seth said it was time to break for lunch.

We moved from the meeting table to another part of the stage, where we had a cardboard box cut and painted to look like a barbeque fire pit. The audience cracked up again when I asked Analise what she was having for lunch, and she said "leftovers" and held up a giant turkey leg we had cut out of cardboard. Then, when we all roasted our lunches over the open fire pit, the audience laughed even more.

"Wow," I thought to myself. "We might actually win this thing."

I didn't think it for very long. Evan and his gang's skit went last, and theirs was more like a professional Broadway show than an OMG skit. It was crazy. First all the lights in the auditorium went dark, and there was this flashing green spotlight zipping all over the stage. Somehow they managed to get smoke to fill up the stage (I found out later they used a barrel of dry ice and a fan), and they had loud space-age sounding music coming from speakers that they had set up all over the auditorium. It was like a laser light show.

Then the lights came up and the stage looked like someone's living room, with a couch and chairs and a coffee table and lamp and whatnot. Evan was sitting in this big lounge chair, and he was dressed up to look like someone's dad, with a coat and tie and wool pants and a pillow in his shirt to make him look chubby. He even had a fake moustache on and his hair was all greased down flat. Two of Evan's buddies were dressed like little kids, with high-water pants and suspenders and those little beanie-type hats that kids wore like fifty years ago. They were sitting on the couch and pretending to watch TV, while Evan was pretending to read a newspaper.

A girl pretending to be the mom of the family yelled from offstage that it was time to walk the dino dog. The two kids argued about whose turn it was, and finally Evan said they'd better stop arguing and do it. But the kids complained that they always get dragged along the street when they do it, so Evan said fine, he'd do it, just so they would stop arguing. So Evan whistled for the dino dog and called, "Here, boy."

Some more smoke came from offstage, and this loud classical music that almost sounded like a thunderstorm was playing. And then this massive thing rolled onto the stage – it was a giant plaster model of an animal that had the body of a dog and the head of a dinosaur, and it was seriously about ten feet tall. The whole audience gasped when they saw it. It was the dino dog.

The idea of course was that dinosaurs never became extinct and instead got turned into pets. There was a lot more to Evan's group's skit, including a song that they all sang about what a good pet a dino dog made, because it was fun to ride and play with, blah blah blah, and it had some funny lines in it about dino dogs knocking over furniture and how hard it was to clean up after them when they went to the bathroom. But the giant dino dog itself was the most awesome thing about their skit. It was painted green and very realistic looking, and it was sitting on top of a wooden frame with wheels so that it could roll right across the stage. Plus they had rigged it up with a tape recorder tied around its neck, so that when Evan talked to it he could press a button and it would make a really loud bark, sort of like a cross between a bark and a roar. And the yellow eyes lit up when it barked, and then Evan pressed another button and it made a panting sound, like dogs make, and more smoke came out of its mouth. I thought that seemed more like a dragon than a dinosaur, but no one else seemed to notice. It was too cool.

When the skit ended and the audience went crazy clapping and hooting and stamping their feet, I knew it was all over for Team Electricity. There was no way we could beat that.

Mr. Van Vleck climbed back up onto the stage and made his way to the microphone.

"Thank you all for coming to this year's performance of the Olympic Mind Games," he said. "The judging is complete, and I will announce the winner in just a few minutes. Please relax and stay in your seats – I'll be with you shortly."

The reason Van Vleck didn't announce the winner right then is because of the OMG tradition called "reflection." What happens is, right after the end of the performances Van Vleck gathers all the kids backstage who were in the skits and asks each team a few questions, about whether we had a good time and if we learned anything and stuff like that. The idea is for us to remember that OMG is more about learning and having fun than it is about winners and losers. When we were little kids in first grade, we totally bought into it when Van Vleck said all of that stuff to us. Now, we just wanted him to get on with it so we could find out who won.

All the kids gathered around Mr. Van Vleck in a big circle, kind of clumped together in our teams. Van Vleck hunched down so that he could look directly into our eyes, and started asking each team his four questions about our OMG experience. The first question was, "Did you have fun?" The second question was, "Did you learn anything from participating in OMG?" The third question was, "Did every member of your team get a chance to participate?" And the last question was, "Did any adults give you direct help with your performance?" Mr. Van Vleck had to ask us that last question, because OMG is a big national competition that has rules set by a group of school principals, and one of the rules is that parents and other grownups aren't allowed to help the kids with their performances – it's supposed to be a kid-only project.

Van Vleck started with Team Movie Stars. They admitted that only two members of the team did any of the work, which was no big surprise considering how lame their skit was. That wasn't against the rules so they didn't get in real trouble, although Mr. Van Vleck told them that next time they should be sure to include everyone. Also no big surprise, they did not have any help from their parents. If they had, we all would have worried about those parents.

We were next. Van Vleck hunched down and looked each of us in the eye.

"So, Team Electricity," he asked, "did you all have fun?"

"We definitely had fun," Tibby volunteered. "But we also fought a lot."

"Sounds like you learned that it's not always easy to work together, is it?" Van Vleck asked.

"We sure did," Seth answered. "It's especially hard when everyone has to tell the truth all the time."

Mr. Van Vleck laughed. "And did everyone participate?" he asked.

"We did," Analise whispered. "All of us."

"Very good," Van Vleck said. "And what about grownups – did any help you out?"

"My mom drove us to get fabric," Analise said.

"And she taught us how to sew our costumes," I admitted.

"Hmmm," Van Vleck said, stroking his beard. "Well, Analise, did your mother actually sew the costumes?"

"No," Analise answered. "She just taught us how."

"Look," Seth said, turning one side edge of his toga inside out so that Van Vleck could see the jagged stitches and collection of safety pins holding it together. "I sewed it myself."

Mr. Van Vleck bent down to take a closer look and Seth pulled up his costume, so that Van Vleck could see the stitching. Then we all heard a ripping sound. The next thing we knew, Seth was standing there in his boxer shorts, a piece of toga in each hand.

Van Vleck laughed. "It sure looks like you sewed it yourself," he said. "I'll take your word for it." He explained that it was okay for parents to show us how to do things, they just weren't supposed to do the things for us. So having Analise's mom teach us to sew wasn't against the rules. We were in the clear.

Mr. Van Vleck ran through the four questions with all the other teams. Evan and the rest of Team Dino Dogs were last.

"Your performance was very enjoyable," Van Vleck told Evan. "The special effects were very impressive. Did you have fun?"

"Yeah," Evan said. "It was awesome. Making the smoke was really cool."

"That's good," Van Vleck said. "Sounds like you had a built-in science lesson. Was that part of what you learned from the experience?"

"Yeah," one of Evan's buddies said. "Science. And how to make smoke."

"Excellent," Van Vleck said. "And was every member of your team involved?"

The smallest boy on the team, one with dark hair hanging over his eyes, raised his hand. "I didn't get to make any smoke," he said. Evan jabbed him with his elbow.

"Oh, you didn't?" Mr. Van Vleck asked the boy. "Well, did you get to participate in other ways."

"Sure," the boy admitted. "I painted some scenery and stuff. And I got to be one of the kids in the skit." Evan grinned.

"Well, that sounds fine," Mr. Van Vleck said. "And to you, team captain of Team Dino Dogs," he said to Evan, "one last question: Did you have any help from grownups?"

Evan opened his mouth to reply, but the only thing that came out was a kind of low groan. It sounded like he was in pain. He shook his head and tried again, but again only a moaning sound came out. His mouth started to smile but then it flattened out again, and his eyes got watery.

"Tell me Evan," Van Vleck said, more sternly this time, "did you have any help from grownups?"

Evan's shoulders slumped. "Yes, Principal Van Vleck," he said softly. "Yes we did."

"Who helped you?" Van Vleck asked.

"My dad," Evan said. "And mom. And his dad and mom," he said, pointing to one of the other boys on his team. "And . . . well, just about all our moms and dads."

"And what exactly did they help you with?"

"My dad built the big dino dog in his workshop," Evan explained. "And my mom wrote the script to our skit, and our song. And the other parents made our costumes and painted most of the scenery. And taught us how to make smoke with dry ice."

"I see," Van Vleck said, standing up straight. "Well then, Evan," he asked slowly, "what exactly did you kids do?"

"I wrote a joke for the skit," Evan said. "But my mom said we had to cut it out. Because it was about dinosaur poop."

One of the other boys on the team, the one with hair covering his eyes, spoke up. "It was my idea to wear a sweater vest," he said.

Mr. Van Vleck sighed. "Anything else?" He asked. "Anything else at all?" Team Dino Dogs all shook their heads. "Well, this is very serious," Mr. Van Vleck said, pulling on his beard. "Very serious indeed."

CHAPTER NINETEEN

Principal Van Vleck spent a full five minutes huddled with Ms. Gleason, whispering and looking at the score sheets. The audience was getting squirmy, and the auditorium felt like it was ten degrees hotter than five minutes before. Finally Van Vleck made his way slowly along the side aisle until he came to the stage, and then he crept up the steps. He tapped the microphone a few times with his finger and then cleared his throat.

"I'm sorry for the delay, everyone," Van Vleck said, and his voice seemed shaky. "There's been a bit of a . . . complication."

The crowd started to mumble a bit, but Van Vleck kept going. "I won't get into all the details right now," he said, "but one of the teams has been disqualified."

It sounded like the entire audience sucked in their breath in one huge gasp. Nothing like this had ever happened at OMG before. "In any case," Van

Vleck continued, "let's get on with the awarding of the trophy."

Ms. Gleason rushed to the edge of the stage and handed up a small gold-colored statue to Principal Van Vleck. The trophy was a copy of a famous statue of a man sitting on a tree stump or something with his head resting on his chin. It was supposed to mean that the winners of OMG were really smart, I think. I wanted it badly. All of us did – Seth, Tibby, Analise and I, and I'm sure all the members of the other teams too. After Team Dino Dogs' performance it looked like we had no chance, but then that issue of Evan's parents helping came up. Could this be Team Electricity's year?

"The winner of this year's Olympic Mind Games competition," Van Vleck said, his voice stronger now, "is . . . Team Electricity!"

About half the audience exploded in a cheer. Seth jumped up and pumped his fist in the air, and I shouted "Yes!", while Tibby and Analise hugged each other. The other half of the audience groaned. After the clapping died down, I saw a man in the middle of the second row of the auditorium stand up. His forehead was crinkled up and he looked like he was grinding his teeth. He did not look happy.

"Excuse me, Principal Van Vleck," the man said loudly. "I'm Ernie Boynton. Evan Boynton's father. I'm sorry to break up the celebration, but something's not right here. My son's team, Team Dino Dogs, clearly gave the best performance. No question about it. I mean, you'd have to be blind, deaf and dumb not to see that."

"Well," Van Vleck said, "these things are always a matter of opinion. I'm sorry if you're disappointed."

"I'm not disappointed," Evan's dad said, even louder, "I'm outraged. My son's team was the best team. The only explanation for why they didn't win is you must have disqualified them. Is that what happened? Did you disqualify Team Dino Dogs?"

The whole crowd started rumbling. Mr. Van Vleck put up his hands to calm them down, and opened his mouth to say something. I expected him to say that what went on in the OMG reflection circle – where Van Vleck asked us the questions and we told him about our experience – was for the kids to know only, not the adults. But Van Vleck's face went pale and his eyes glazed over, and this is what he whispered into the microphone instead: "Yes. Yes, I did disqualify Team Dino Dogs."

"What on earth did you do that for?" Mr. Boynton shouted.

"The team members admitted to me that they had help," Van Vleck said. "From you, actually. And other adults."

"That's ridiculous!" Boynton said.

"The kids told me themselves," Van Vleck explained.

"Well," Boynton said, "so what? So what if they had a little help? I'm sure every team had some help from parents."

"A little bit of help, possibly," Van Vleck admitted. "But nothing like the help Team Dino Dogs received, I'm afraid."

Mr. Boynton's face was the color of a tomato now, and he looked like he might burst. "Oh, is that right?" he said. "Is that right? Well, tell me this: who exactly are you to make that decision? Who are you to take that trophy away from my son?"

"I'm the principal of this school, Mr. Boynton," Van Vleck said. "It's my job to make those decisions."

"Oh yeah?" Boynton said, his voice echoing off the walls. "Well, who the heck made you principal anyway? I don't remember voting for you."

"The school board makes that decision," Van Vleck answered. "And the Superintendent, of course."

It looked like Mr. Boynton was beaten now. His wife was tugging on his sleeve, trying to get him to sit down, and the rest of the crowd seemed to be behind Van Vleck now. Boynton started to crouch, like he was going to drop back down in his seat, but then he changed his mind and tried one more argument. "So if we never voted for you," he said, "how do we know you're qualified for the job? How do we know you're qualified to disqualify my son, or make any other decisions for that matter?"

Van Vleck stroked his beard. "I suppose you don't know," he admitted.

"Well," Boynton said, thinking maybe he had an opening, "are you? Are you qualified to make these decisions? Are you qualified to be principal of George Washington Elementary School?"

And with that question, everything changed. The tables turned on Principal Van Vleck. "To be perfectly honest," he said, barely louder than a whisper. "I'm not."

Even Mr. Boynton seemed surprised. "What did you say?" he said.

"I said, I'm not qualified to make these decisions," Van Vleck repeated. "You're right. I'm not qualified to be your principal. I'm a fraud. I'm a phony. I'm a fake. I'm . . . sorry." Van Vleck rushed down the stage stairs, through the center aisle of the auditorium and out the back door.

The audience was silent. After a minute or so, Mr. Boynton broke into a wide grin. "Pretty interesting, huh everyone?" he said. "I'll bet the Superintendent will be interested to hear what Van Vleck just said."

CHAPTER TWENTY

No time to celebrate our victory. Without even thinking about it or talking to each other, Tibby, Seth, Analise and I raced after Principal Van Vleck. We had no idea why he said he was a phony, and to be honest we didn't even care. He was a great principal and he was in trouble, so we wanted to find out if we could help.

We caught up with Van Vleck back at his office. He was sitting at his desk, his head hanging down over his mess of papers and his hands covering his face. He didn't seem to even notice when the four of us came barging through the door.

Analise came up to the front of his desk. "Principal Van Vleck," she said in a whisper. "Are you okay?"

Van Vleck took his hands off his face and looked up at her. He gave her a tired smile, the kind of smile someone gives his family in a movie when really he's dying but he wants everyone to think he's going to be fine. "You're very sweet to ask," Van Vleck said. "I'm sure I'll be fine. Eventually."

"What's going on?" I asked him. "Why did you say you were a phony back there?"

Van Vleck looked at me. "Because I am," he said, and then he just looked down at the floor.

"What do you mean?" Seth pressed. "What are you being a phony about?"

Van Vleck gave a long, deep sigh. Then he stroked his beard a few times, and smiled that weak smile again. "I might as well tell you kids," he said. He cleared his throat. "About five years ago," he explained, "I was doing some genealogy research."

"Why were you doing research about genies?" Seth asked.

Van Vleck chuckled. "Genealogy isn't the study of genies," he explained. "It means studying your own family, your family tree."

"Oh," Seth said, blushing. Tibby rolled her eyes.

"Anyway," Van Vleck continued, "as I'm sure you all know, the Van Vleck family has a long and distinguished history in this town. In particular, Octavius Van Vleck is one of our town's great historical figures."

"And he was your great great great great great grandfather, or something," I said.

"That's what I thought," Van Vleck said. "But recently when I looked at some old birth certificates and marriage records, it became clear to me that I was not, in fact, a direct descendant of Octavius Van Vleck. Instead, my family line can be traced up to Octavius' younger brother, Hector Van Vleck."

"Who was he?" Tibby asked.

"He was no Octavius, that's for sure," Van Vleck explained. "He was kind of a drifter and a cheat, the black sheep of the family. He lived in a small log cabin at the edge of town, and at one point he found a small circle of perfectly round, smooth rocks in a clearing in the woods behind his house. There's some question of whether Hector had actually gone crazy by then or if he was just a swindler, but in any event he told lots of townspeople about his discovery. He tried to convince them that the rock circle was some kind of holy spot, and he even invented his own religion based on it and tried to recruit people from town to join."

"Then what happened?" Analise asked.

"Well," Van Vleck continued, "a few of the townspeople came to look at his rock circle. One of the men picked up a rock, felt it, sniffed it, and then dropped it back on the ground. Turns out it wasn't a rock at all."

"What was it?" Seth asked.

Van Vleck smiled and shook his head. "Petrified deer poop." He laughed at the thought of it. "I'm not the direct descendant of the founder of Honestyville. I came from a man who tried to start a religion based on deer droppings."

"But you're still part of the Van Vleck family," I said, trying to comfort him. "They built this town. Who cares if your actual great great great great great grandfather was kind of wacky? Your great great great great great uncle was the town hero."

"That's another thing," Van Vleck said. "I did some more research into the history of our town, and the Van Vleck family's role in it." He shook his head. "It's not as rosy a picture as we all thought. The whole story, that the Van Vlecks gave the Native Americans a fair deal for the land – that's actually based on a misprint in the original town charter. I found some photocopies of pages of Octavius Van Vleck's diary. It turns out that he paid the Native Americans about thirty-nine dollars for the land, plus some glass beads that he told them were very expensive but really were cheap. He didn't give them a fair deal at all. He was a phony. Just like me."

We all stood there silently for a minute.

"Then it's not just you," Tibby said, breaking the silence.

"What do you mean?" Van Vleck asked.

"It's not just you who's a phony," she explained. "It's all of us. The whole town. We all think we're such a great town because we gave the Native Americans a fair deal. But we didn't. We're no better than Hector Van Vleck. Worse maybe – our whole town's been living a lie for hundreds of years. We shouldn't be called Honestyville at all. Out town should be called Cheaterville."

Just then Van Vleck's phone rang. He picked it up, and his face went white. "Oh, hello Superintendent Becker. . . . Yes, yes I did . . . that's right, after the performance . . . okay, sure . . . of course, tomorrow is fine . . . all right, goodbye." He hung up.

"I guess the Superintendent heard about tonight," I said.

Van Vleck nodded. "I'm surprised it took this long," he said. "He's coming to see me. Tomorrow."

"That doesn't sound too good," Seth said.

"No, it doesn't," Van Vleck agreed.

"Do you think he'll fire you?" Analise whispered.

"I can't imagine he won't," Van Vleck answered.

Things seemed pretty bleak at that moment, but then I got an idea. "All this stuff about the real history of Honestyville," I said, "everyone in school really ought to know it. Don't you think? As, like, an educational thing?"

"I guess they should," Van Vleck agreed.

"Well then, you should tell them about it. Tomorrow."

"With Superintendent Becker coming to visit?" Van Vleck asked.

"Yes," I said. "It's the perfect time. We should have an assembly. Everyone in this whole school – in this whole town, really – is living a lie, just like Tibby said. Not just you. We've all got secrets, including this one big one. When it comes out, the Superintendent will see that yours is no worse than anyone's. Maybe he won't fire you."

"You should hold an assembly," Tibby added. "For the whole school. You can tell everyone the truth about Honestyville. And the Superintendent."

"An honesty assembly," Analise whispered.

"I don't know," Van Vleck said, stroking his beard.

"Come on," Seth said. "What have you got to lose?"

"You always say that we should know our history," Tibby said. "Don't you think the whole school should know what really happened when Honestyville first became a town? The real, true story?"

"I suppose so," Van Vleck agreed, even though he was shaking his head. "All right then – an honesty assembly it is. I might be humiliated and get fired, but at least our school will know the truth. Maybe something good will come out of all of this after all."

CHAPTER TWENTY ONE

For the first time in my life, I was excited about going to an assembly. Usually they're incredibly boring – they have some lame topic, like safety or kindness or something like that, and some grownup talks to us about it like we're all in kindergarten. Like we don't know that we should keep our shoes tied, or that we shouldn't tease other kids if they're fat or talk weird or whatnot. Anyway, I'm sure the topic for this assembly – honesty – sounded just as lame as safety and kindness to the other kids in school, but I knew this assembly would be an especially good one.

It was scheduled to start at ten o'clock in the morning, which was the same time that Superintendent Becker was coming to talk to Principal Van Vleck. Van Vleck didn't want to to do it that way – he thought it would seem rude to make the Superintendent wait through an assembly before they had their talk. But I convinced Van Vleck that the whole point was for the Superintendent to hear what he had to say at the assembly, and besides, if they met before it started Becker might go ahead and fire Van Vleck on the spot, and then the whole plan would have been for nothing. So ten o'clock it was.

All the kids filed into the auditorium, one grade at a time starting with the kindergarteners who sat in the front two rows. That was one good thing about being in fourth grade – we got to sit toward the back of the auditorium, which meant that when an assembly got really boring at least we could whisper to each other or pass notes to keep ourselves entertained. Mrs. Groom didn't even get mad at us when we did it, as long as we were quiet about it, because she understood how boring these assemblies were.

This time, though, I was paying close attention. Van Vleck was already standing on stage behind the microphone, stroking his beard and looking pretty jumpy. I noticed a large, bald man in a dark suit and red tie enter the auditorium from one of the side doors, and I assumed that he was Superintendent Becker. His skin was shiny and very pink, and he had a stubby nose and little eyes surrounded by crinkles and a large sticking-out belly. The whole effect was that he looked like a cross between a human and a pig, stuffed into a business suit. He started to walk toward the stage, probably to talk to Mr. Van Vleck, but then the lights went down and all the kids got quiet, and he realized the assembly was about to start. So he squeezed himself into a seat along the far aisle and waited, like the rest of us.

"Good morning everyone," Van Vleck said into the microphone. It made that awful screeching sound, and we all covered our ears. "Sorry about that," Van Vleck said, moving a few inches back. "There, that's better." He cleared his throat. "The theme of today's assembly, as you all know, is honesty. You've all heard me talk about the history of Honestyville, about my proud Van Vleck ancestors settling this town, and about the fair deal that they gave the Native Americans who lived here before them. Well, the time has come for you to learn the truth. The truth about Honestyville. The truth about the Van Vleck family. And the truth about me."

The kids all got very quiet. So quiet, in fact, that we could hear Ms. Gleason making a wheezing sound all the way in the front of the auditorium. It made me wonder if all this stuff with Principal Van Vleck might literally cause her to have a heart attack or something. To my surprise, I started to actually feel bad for her.

Van Vleck went through the whole story he told us the night before: that his real ancestor was Hector Van Vleck, the whack-job crook who tried to start a religion based on a circle of pertified deer poop; that Octavius Van Vleck wasn't quite the hero everyone believed him to be; and that Honestyville actually was founded on a swindle of the Native Americans, not a fair deal at all.   When he was finished, Van Vleck took a deep breath and broke into a smile. "Well then," he said. "That's the truth. All of it. I know I'll probably be fired before the end of the day" – he looked at Superintendent Becker when he said this – "but I don't care.   I feel great.   My conscience is clear.   It's like a weight has been lifted from my shoulders."   Then he paused and his eyebrows went up. "In fact," he said to all of us in the audience, "you should all try it.   Come up here and tell the truth. You won't believe how good it feels."

Nobody moved. We weren't sure if Van Vleck really was asking us to come up on stage or what. Had he gone completely crazy?

Van Vleck turned to Ms. Gleason in the front row. "Come on up here, Ms. Gleason!" he shouted. He sounded like the host of a game show. "You must have something you'd like to get off your chest."

Ms. Gleason looked totally embarrassed, but she climbed up the steps to the stage. Van Vleck said to her, "So Rhoda" – I guess that's Ms. Gleason's first name – "tell us: what secret do you have in your heart that you wish you could say out in the open?"

Van Vleck pushed the microphone in front of Ms. Gleason's face. Her eyes went glassy and her cheeks seemed to fall. "What I've been holding inside

all these years," she said, her voice quivering, "is that
. . . I love you, Principal Van Vleck. And I don't want
you to get fired. I don't know how I'd get up each
morning without knowing I'd see you!" She started
to sob.

Van Vleck put his arm around Ms. Gleason's
shoulders. "There, there, Rhoda," he said. "I'm
flattered, I really am. And I'm very fond of you as
well." Then his face brightened. "All right!" he
shouted. "Who's next?"

The teachers all looked at Mr. Lewis. He was
the guidance counselor, so I guess it was his job to get
involved in whatever touchy-feely thing was going on
at school. Mr. Lewis shrugged and made his way up
the steps to the stage.

"Excellent!" Van Vleck said. "All right then,
Robin" – we were learning a lot of teachers' first
names today – "what is it that you'd like to tell us?
What secret has been weighing you down?"

Mr. Lewis breathed into the microphone.
"Comic books," he said in his usual soft voice. "I read
comic books. Every night before I go to bed. My
favorite is Spider Man."

For some reason, all of us kids started
clapping when his said this. I'm not sure why –
maybe just to break the silence. Anyway, it seemed
to make both Van Vleck and Mr. Lewis very happy.

Van Vleck patted him on the back. "That's wonderful!" he said. "Don't you feel light as air now?"

"I do," Mr. Lewis said. "I really do." He started to step away from the microphone, but then he stopped and leaned back to it. "Also, I wear Spider Man pajamas!" he said. The whole audience went wild, whooping and clapping and stamping our feet.

Then one kid in the middle of the auditorium, a third grader I didn't recognize, jumped out of his seat and shouted "I wet my bed at night!" We all clapped even louder.

Another kid, a fifth grade girl sitting on the other side of the aisle from me, stood up and said, "I keep all my toenail clippings in a glass jar next to my bed!" The whole crowd roared and stamped even more. The clapping and hooting got louder and louder until the whole room felt like it was shaking.

And then, over the noise of the crowd, one deep, booming voice shouted, "Enough!"

The auditorium went silent. I looked over toward the side of the auditorium where the voice came from. Superintendent Becker was standing up, his huge body towering like a statue over the kids sitting around him. His bald head was sweaty and his face was red, and he was panting like he had just run in a race.

"That . . . is . . . enough!" he shouted again, although by now no one was saying anything. Becker stomped toward the stage and up the steps. He stood in front of Principal Van Vleck, so that their faces were only a foot apart.

"This school," the Superintendent said slowly, "is a disgrace.   Teachers who wear Spider Man pajamas. Students who wet the bed. And worst of all, a principal who pretends to be someone he's not, and insults the founders of our great town. I will not stand for it. And thank goodness I am in a position to do something about it. Principal Van Vleck," he said, his beady eyes narrowing, "you are dismissed. You have thirty minutes to clean out your desk and be out of the building, or I'll call security."

Van Vleck hung his head down and shuffled toward the stage steps. Ms. Gleason sobbed.

"This school disgusts me," Superintendent Becker continued to say.   He was next to the microphone so we all could hear every word. "I mean, for God's sake," he added, "this entire building smells like rotten onions. What on earth are you serving the children for lunch?"

I jumped out of my seat. "Wait!" I screamed. Van Vleck froze. Every head turned toward me. Superintendent Becker scoured the audience to see where the voice had come from.

"Mr. Superintendent, sir," I said. "You must have something you want to say that you've never told anyone before. A secret."

"Don't be ridiculous," Becker said, finding me with his eyes. "Sit down and shut your mouth immediately."

Ask him a direct question, I told myself. I tried again, using the same words Van Vleck had used earlier to get Ms. Gleason talking. "Mr. Becker, what secret do you have in your heart that you wish you could tell us all?"

Becker's face went from red and twisted up to calm and expressionless. "Yes," he whispered into the microphone. "Yes, I do have a secret. I do have something I'd like to say."

Tibby stood up next to me. "Tell us!" she shouted. "You can tell us. We won't laugh at you."

"Okay." Becker cleared his throat. "I have a collection," he said into the microphone. "Of dolls. Antique dolls. Antique Barbie dolls, from the 1970s." Tears began streaming down his cheeks. "Each with an original outfit. A roller derby Barbie. A disco nights Barbie. An airline stewardess Barbie." He was really crying now. "A cheerleader Barbie."

Mr. Van Vleck went back over to him and put a hand on his shoulder. "It's okay," Van Vleck said. "Let it out."

"My mother never let me have Barbies as a child," Becker said between sobs. "She said they were for girls. But I wanted them so badly."

Tibby and I started clapping, and then Seth and Analise joined us, and soon the whole audience was standing and clapping for Superintendent Becker. Someone shouted out, "If you wanted Barbies, you should have been allowed to have them!"

"Thank you," Becker answered. "Thank you all." He wiped his nose on his sleeve. "You are a wonderful bunch of students. Really wonderful. Van Vleck," he said, turning to our Principal, "you have a wonderful group of students here after all."

"They are a good bunch of kids," Van Vleck said.

"Whatever you're doing here," Becker continued, "it's working. These are some fine, fine students. And this is a fine assembly. Really a wonderful idea. I haven't felt this good in years. You keep up the good work."

"Does that mean I'm not fired?" Van Vleck asked.

Becker smiled. "It sure does." The audience cheered. "On one condition, though."

"What is it?" Van Vleck asked.

"You have to promise me that you'll hold an Honesty Assembly every year. And that you'll invite me back for each one."

Van Vleck stuck out his hand. "It's a deal," he said.

Becker took his hand and shook it. "Excellent," he said, clapping Van Vleck on the back. "I'll be going on my way now. I don't think we need to have that talk after all. Everything looks to be in fine shape here at George Washington Elementary. I'll see you – and you kids, too – next year!"

CHAPTER TWENTY TWO

Things got better at home, too. That afternoon when Johna and I got off the school bus we saw Mom pulling into the driveway. It was a weird sight, because usually she didn't come home until much later. Even weirder, she had a big smile on her face. Not that it was strange in general for my mom to smile, but in the last couple of weeks she and my dad hadn't been smiling much, so Johna and I definitely noticed.

We jogged up to the house and caught Mom just as she was going in.

"You're home early," I called to her.

"I am," Mom said, still smiling. "I moved around some client meetings so I could surprise your dad," she explained. "Hey Johna, you don't have any plans tonight, do you?"

"Nope," Johna said.

"Great. Do you think you could stay home and look after Paulie? I couldn't get a babysitter on such short notice."

"Sure, Mom," Johna said.

Usually I would tell my mom that I'm not a baby and I don't need Johna to "watch" me, but I was too curious about what she had planned even to complain. "What are you guys doing tonight?" I asked.

"It's a surprise," Mom said, wagging her eyebrows. We all went into the house.

Dad was in his studio. Mom knocked on the door and then opened it a crack, just enough so she could stick her mouth through it and say, "I'm home, Andrew. Come on out to the kitchen when you have a minute."

We followed Mom to the kitchen. She was humming as she pulled the milk out of the refrigerator and poured Johna and me each a glass, and then took the cookies down from the cabinet. The humming was another weird sign, but a good one.

Dad appeared a couple of minutes later, while Johna and I were eating our snack. He had his painty work clothes on, and his hands were behind his back. "You're home early," he said to my mom suspiciously.

"I have a surprise for you," Mom said. She opened up her pocket book and pulled out an envelope, which she handed to Dad.

Dad tore the envelope open and pulled out two tickets. His eyes widened as he looked at them.

"They're for the extreme fighting match," he said. "For tonight."

"Bone Crusher Bernard against the Murderous Monk," Mom explained.

"And you and I are going together?" Dad asked.

"That's right," Mom said. She put her arms around Dad and kissed him. "It's my way of apologizing for being such an inflexible, controlling jerk. I'm sorry. And I figure I ought to learn a little more about this extreme fighting business before I judge it."

Dad smiled. "Well, I guess we'll have to wait for another night to watch this then." He pulled out a DVD he was holding behind his back and handed it to Mom.

"It's Star Trek," Mom said, grinning at him.

"The complete first and second seasons," Dad explained. "I'm sorry too. For going behind your back about the extreme fighting." They kissed again.

"This is all very nice," I said, "but I think that's enough kissing."

"Seriously," Johna said. "You're creeping us out."

"Fine," Mom said. "Well just have to make out later. At the extreme fighting match."

"I'm sure Bone Crusher Bernard and the Murderous Monk won't mind," Dad said, winking at me.

CHAPTER TWENTY THREE

So that's it. That's what happened that time when the truck went into the lake. You can believe every word of it, because I wrote it all down while everything still smelled like rotten onions.

Four days after my Mom and Dad went to the extreme fighting match, the truth serum wore off. We were at school, in our classroom, lining up to go to the cafeteria. Mrs. Groom opened the classroom door, and we all smelled a wave of hot dog odor, like a warm breeze blowing across our faces. It's not like hot dog smell is the best smell in the world, but our class acted like it was, jumping up and down and cheering. Finally, something didn't smell like rotten onions.

I turned to Seth, and we high fived. "That's a relief," he said. Now people will stop telling the truth all the time. Everything will get back to normal."

Seth was sort of right. Teachers stopped telling each other their deep dark secrets, kids stopped confessing their crimes, and Evan went back to being a jerk on the playground. But everything wasn't exactly the same as before the truth serum. People seemed a little more careful around each other, a little bit nicer I guess. We all knew that we all had secrets, every one of us. It kind of made us all equal somehow, knowing that teachers worried about how they looked and kids still wet their beds and that we all had some weird habits. Back when the truth serum was working on us, it felt good to get some of our secrets out in the open, but now that it had worn off, we were all pretty relieved to keep this stuff to ourselves. So the school had a new kind of quiet, with everybody respecting each other's privacy just a little more than we had before.

Not everything worked out so great, though. When my mom found out about that email from Susan – remember, the one about the truth serum – and how I read it, and erased it, I got in serious trouble. I won't get into all the bloody details, but let's just say I won't be playing Defender or any other computer games for a long, long time. Or getting my allowance. Or watching TV. And I think I'm still alive only because my parents were in a good mood.

You're probably also wondering if Tibby and I ever went out on our date, and if we did, how it all went. Well, I'm not telling. Because I don't smell rotten onions anymore, so I don't have to. Even if

you, or anyone else for that matter, asks me a direct
question about it.